Unruly Catholic Nuns

Unruly Catholic Nuns

Sisters' Stories

Edited by

Jeana DelRosso, Leigh Eicke, and Ana Kothe

excelsior editions
State University of New York Press
Albany, New York

Published by State University of New York Press, Albany

Excelsior Editions is an imprint of State University of New York Press

For information, contact State University of New York Press, Albany, NY
www.sunypress.edu

Production by Eileen Nizer
Marketing by Kate R. Seburyamo

Library of Congress Cataloging-in-Publication Data

Names: DelRosso, Jeana, editor.
Title: Unruly Catholic nuns : sisters' stories / edited by Jeana DelRosso, Leigh Eicke, and Ana Kothe.
Description: Albany, NY : State University of New York, 2017. | Series: Excelsior editions | Includes bibliographical references and index.
Identifiers: LCCN 2016047190 (print) | LCCN 2017028603 (ebook) | ISBN 9781438466491 (ebook) | ISBN 9781438466477 (hardcover : alk. paper) | ISBN 9781438466484 (pbk. : alk. paper)
Subjects: LCSH: Women in the Catholic Church. | Nuns—Biography.
Classification: LCC BX2347.8.W6 (ebook) | LCC BX2347.8.W6 U57 2017 (print) | DDC 271/.90073—dc23
LC record available at https://lccn.loc.gov/2016047190

10 9 8 7 6 5 4 3 2 1

To Unruly Sisters Everywhere

≈

Contents

Acknowledgments and Permissions   xi

Introduction: On Unruly Nuns (and the Women Who
Admire Them)   1

Part One: Our Father Wills

The Nun Speaks to Her Church   11
  Julia Rice, OSF

God Shoes   14
  Jeannine Gramick, SL

She, with the Alabaster Jar   25
  Victoria Marie

The Chancery   27
  Jean Molesky-Poz

No One Has Hired Us   34
  Ann Breslin

Pain Cries to a Patriarchal Church   38
  Mary Ellen Rufft, CDP
    The Altered Boy   38
    A Pillar of Power   39
    Only a Stone   40

Crooked Since Birth   41
Twice-Broken Vows   42
Bed or Bread?   43
A Resurrection   45

Part Two: Our Mother Works

Sister Dorothy Stang, Assassinated   49
   Liz Dolan

Unruly Women: Nuns Out of Order   50
   Carole Ganim

Journey to Unruliness   60
   Pat Montley

The Renunciation   69
   Pat Montley

Polishing the Brass   77
   Liz Dolan

Timing   83
   Patricia M. Dwyer

I am a Catholic Nun   89
   Sharon Kanis, SSND

Faith in the Wasteland   93
   Christine Schenk, CSJ

Part Three: The Holy Spirit Confirms

& The Truth Shall Set U Free   113
   Jane Morrissey, SSJ

Sisters behind Walls   132
   Paula Timpson

Rose Hawthorne Creates   133
    Liz Dolan

When Grief Opens the Doors to the Sacred   134
    Michele Birch-Conery

Notes on Contributors   141

Acknowledgments
and Permissions

The editors would like to thank the following individual and press for allowing us to republish the piece we have included in this volume:

Pat Montley originally published "The Renunciation" as the last scene from *Bible Herstory,* Samuel French, 1975.

Introduction

On Unruly Nuns
(and the Women Who Admire Them)

Go calmly in peace, for you will have a good escort, because He Who created you has sent you the Holy Spirit and has always guarded you as a mother does her child who loves her.

—St. Clare of Assisi[1]

St. Clare, one of the first followers of Saint Francis of Assisi, founded the order that is now known as Poor Ladies, a monastic religious order for women in the Franciscan tradition. She wrote their Rule of Life—the first monastic rule known to have been written by a woman. To do this, she had to resist the rules and efforts of her father, a noble and wealthy man. Her words make clear not only an understanding of a female feature of God but also the active role of women in the church.

When we began to think about the next book in our Unruly Catholic Women Writers series, we knew exactly whom we wanted to represent, what stories we wanted to relate, which voices we wanted to make heard: religious women. We wanted to tell the Sisters' stories, which we knew were out there. We also knew exactly what—and whom—we were referring to when we were thinking of unruly nuns, although the nuns we reached out to frequently did not see themselves in such a way. One told us she wasn't unruly enough to be in our volume; others demurred, saying they had nothing to contribute. Even when they submitted something to us, many Sisters offered disclaimers to their pieces, referring to them as "incomplete" or "a draft" or "just some ideas."

This is characteristic of nuns: unwilling to talk about themselves, unassuming in regard to their own work and abilities, humble to a fault. But we know who they really are. They are S. Simone Campbell, the force behind Nuns on the Bus, addressing social justice issues such as immigration reform and welfare legislation across the United States. They are S. Joan Chittister, whose speech on women's ordination the Vatican tried to silence, but whose order, the Benedictines, asserted that silence was not the Benedictine way. They are S. Teresa Kane, who publicly confronted Pope John Paul II regarding the prohibition against female priesthood—an iconic moment in the history of sisterhood. They are S. Jeannine Gramick, known for her work with the GLBTQ community, who are often ostracized from the Catholic Church.[2] (We are fortunate to include a piece from S. Jeannine here.) They are self-sacrificing. They are unpretentious. They are quietly and without fanfare doing God's business in the world, carrying out small or large tasks, taking care of a child or a nation, performing the work of Christ.

The nuns we know are intelligent, dedicated, often strategic about how best to use resources and how to maneuver around, across, or through the institutional church in order to do the work that God calls them to do. There is the story of one of our colleagues, a nun well into her seventies, still teaching religious studies at a Catholic college. When the bishop issued a directive discouraging theology professors from teaching about women's ordination in the Catholic Church, she gave out the readings on the topic to her students in class and told them to discuss it amongst themselves—and so, therefore, did not technically teach it! This Sister represents the entrepreneurial spirit possessed by so many nuns, as well as their dedication to teaching what is morally right in the face of an often oppressive and discriminatory church.

Recently, Pope Francis has been creating positive change in this historically traditional institution. His focus on issues of social justice is refreshing: he has spoken out against poverty, religious intolerance, environmental destruction, and the church's intense focus on such divisive issues as abortion, contraception, divorce, and homosexuality. He has even signaled his intent to create a commission to study the possibility of allowing women to serve as deacons in the Catholic Church.

However, Pope Francis has not yet moved in the direction of changing papal doctrine on these issues. Moreover, he recently stated that the Roman Catholic Church's teaching that women cannot be ordained as priests is likely to last forever, citing Pope John Paul's position that ordaining women is not possible because Jesus chose only men as his apostles. Pope Francis instead limits women's role to the "feminine dimension" (Brockhaus). And while he has backed down on the Congregation for the Doctrine of the Faith's criticism of the U.S. Leadership Conference of Women Religious, and he has even spoken out against pay inequity for women, these measures are dwarfed by the penultimate patriarchy that is the Roman Catholic Church today, in which nuns can never be priests, women can never hold positions of significant power, and gender inequity remains the rule rather than the exception.

Whether you have faith in him or not, the Pope of the Roman Catholic Church has massive global influence; the importance of the Church on a worldwide scale is unquestionable. Women in the Church are now looking to see to what extent Pope Francis will bring real change to women's lives. But many women religious are not waiting around for his permission to produce the church reforms that many Catholics view as desperately needed and long overdue. They are actively working to secure peace on Earth, rather than asking the needy only to pray to achieve peace in Heaven.

Robert Calderisi, in his exploration of the Catholic Church's role in reaching out to the poor and voiceless around the world, opens his introduction to *Earthly Mission* with a vivid image of the dedication, the sacrifice, and, often, the risk nuns take on a daily basis:

> Somewhere in the developing world, a 57-year-old woman is trudging up a steep hill in the early afternoon, sorry she could not come earlier when it was cooler or delay her visit until the evening. But the person at the top of the

hill needs her urgently [. . .] She is a nurse and a nun, and the woman at the top of the hill may be dying. (3)

Throughout his study, Calderisi discusses countless cases of such nuns, cases that cause him to recommend that a woman become Pope. He asserts that "not everything that it strives to achieve before a woman does finally step out onto the balcony of St. Peter's Basilica should be dismissed as worthless and hypocritical" (9). As his book goes on to show, it is through the work of dedicated, motivated, and often unruly individuals that the Catholic Church has made an impact on addressing inequality and oppression.

We, the editors of this volume, hope to contribute to the global conversation about the role of women religious in the Catholic Church by giving voice to these women and to their unruliness. In our volume, unruliness presents itself in two ways: first, in terms of how Sisters and former Sisters challenge cultural hegemonies and governmental policies or regimes; and, second, in regard to how they challenge the church itself. Many orders of nuns, as well as individual women religious regardless of order, have risked their lives to undertake the struggles of economically and politically oppressed people.[3] Some, like S. Dorothy Stang, have given their lives to protect and give voice to the disenfranchised in Brazil. More recently, S. Lenora Brunetto has risked her life in Brazil to stand up for the landless and environmental devastation brought on by illegal ranching. In a recent interview, the unruly S. Lenora stated that, "As soon as I get time, I want to organize a strike by all the women in the church, all around the world. The church won't function without women" (Cheney 69). She is unafraid.

Such brave women have certainly risked their already marginal position in the church hierarchy. Consider the Maryknoll order of Sisters, who have been fundamental in uniting impoverished women—in the Philippines, for example—and giving them viable and sustainable means to flourish as an alternative to being paid slave wages by multinational corporations. Also consider the School Sisters of Notre Dame, whose primary mission is social justice, with a focus on the education of women and those living in poverty. Clearly, there is great interest in unruly nuns in both secular and religious circles. In these pages, we have collected and published the voices of women who engage in such struggles, and who have articulated these struggles through autobiography and memoir, fiction and nonfiction, poetry and prose. We hope that our book will shed greater light on the works of these Sisters, both in the United States and internationally.

While Pope Francis chose his name in honor of St. Francis of Assisi, who dedicated himself to the poor and who inspired St. Clare to do the same, we the editors see the Sisters in this volume as following the vision of an anchoress who lived and worked not long after these Catholic saints, around the turn of the fifteenth century: Julian of Norwich, the first English woman of letters. Her description and interpretation of her vision in what has come to be called *Showings* offer a conception of the trinity that applies directly to the Sisters in this volume. She writes:

> . . . as truly as God is our Father, so truly is God our Mother. Our Father wills, our Mother works, our good Lord the Holy Spirit confirms. And therefore it is our part to love our God in whom we have our being, reverently thanking and praising him for our creation, mightily praying to our Mother for mercy and pity, and to the Lord the Holy Spirit for help and grace. (296)

We have thus divided the pieces in this volume into three parts, based on Julian's words: "Our Father wills, our Mother works, our good Lord the Holy Spirit confirms." The writings in Part I of this anthology demonstrate, first and foremost, how nuns have followed and continue to pursue the word of God, both in their daily deeds and in how they live their lives. But the will of the Father also reflects the teachings of a male-dominated clergy, against whom many of our contributors have railed, or around whom many have worked. The Father's will is thus depicted paradoxically as both a positive force that can change lives and a hindrance to the good works of the Sisters represented here.

Hence, in Part II, the Mother's work—while the texts herein reference the Blessed Virgin Mary as Mother, they likewise see the face of God as not just father but also Mother, with all the cultural connotations this image evokes. The term "Mother" also invokes the leadership position in Catholic women's religious communities of the Mother Superior, who plays a critical role in the lives of those in her community, as she may either enforce upon her constituents the rule of Rome or encourage in them their unique calling to social justice and mercy. Most significantly, however, Julian's invocation of Mother inserts women into the Holy Trinity, asserting a position for women in church doctrine, just as our contributors assert the value and significance of women in the church.

Finally, in Part III, we include pieces that examine how the Holy Spirit, working through individuals both within and outside the church, confirms the good work that these Sisters have done and continue to do in our neighborhoods, our communities, our nations, and our world, and offers grace and assistance to Sisters in times of trial. The Sisters in this volume are indeed working for God's will, Mother's mercy, and the Holy Spirit's grace. Through them we all can see the light of God's grace on Earth.

Notes

1. These words are widely cited as her own, but they are recorded only in documents from the process of canonization, which show the source is Sisters Filippa and Benvenuta, who shared the words as one prayer of St. Clare's on one of her last days. Sister Filippa asked others to try to remember the words (Armstrong 143).

2. See New Ways Ministry: http://newwaysministry.org/co-founders.html.

3. For example, Mariam Keesy's work for the Justice and Peace Commission in Dar es Salaam, Sister Mary Gabriella's opening of the first credit union for women in the garment industry in South Korea, and Sister Mary Grenough's ambitious social action program for sugar cane workers in the Philippines.

Works Cited

Armstrong, Regis J., OFM, Cap. *Clare of Assisi: Early Documents.* New York/Mahwah, NJ: Paulist Press, 1988.

Brockhaus, Hannah. "Pope Francis Reiterates a Strong 'No' to Women Priests." *Catholic News Agency,* Tuesday, 1 November 2016. http://www.catholicnewsagency.com/news/pope-francis-reiterates-a-strong-no-to-women-priests-71133/.

Calderisi, Robert. *Earthly Mission: The Catholic Church and World Development.* New Haven, CT: Yale UP, 2013.

Campbell, Sister Simone. *A Nun on the Bus: How All of Us Can Create Hope, Change, and Community.* NY: HarperCollins Publishers, 2014.

Cheney, Glen, "Promised Land: Will Brazil's Poor Ever Inherit the Earth?" *Harper's* June 2013, 59–69.

Julian of Norwich. *Showings.* Mahwah, NJ: Paulist Press, 1978.

Part One

Our Father Wills

The Nun Speaks to Her Church

Julia Rice

2009—The Investigation of U.S. Sisters
When I was seventeen,
it was a very good year.
You took me and taught me,
offered me security,
fed me, sheltered me,
veiled me. I passed the hours
praising you, listening.
You kept me close,
and I feared losing you.

When I was thirty-three,
you opened the windows,
you invigorated my work,
deepened my spirit,
taught me to love.
You freed my spirit
to go unchained ways.
Without losing you,
I traveled far,
adventured,
enjoyed the foreign lands
here and far, healing.

Now that I am seventy-five,
you do not trust me.
Suddenly you think
that I have been unfaithful.
I am useless, wrinkled,
worthless to work, worthless to you.
You are so afraid of losing me—
not me, but what I was—
that you take away the shelter,
the food, the clothing,
the learning, the thinking,
the freedom . . .
Are you so embittered now
that you think you know
what to do about me?
Will you now crucify me?

2014—The Results
How little you knew
about your women.
And about what is real.
It was too late to scare me.
How little I knew about
how alike we were across a nation,
across a world.
Our learning, our thinking,
our freedom
are so deeply engrained,
our spirits so united
at a depth you cannot understand,
our faithfulness so firm
you could not move us
anywhere but forward,
away from confining rules.
We are running together
from that cross you planted
to the original Gospel,

to the Jesus who lived
with and for others,
where we find our joy.

God Shoes

Jeannine Gramick

I have been a Roman Catholic nun since 1960. For the first fifteen years of my religious life, my days were spent teaching in grade school, high school, and college. Although I had much professional schooling to prepare me for my teaching career, I learned most from an extracurricular activity that became my full-time ministry for more than forty years. I now look back on my religious life and am grateful for all the learning during these years. I would hardly have thought that a nun would become a specialist in the area of homosexuality, but that is what happened.

Dominic

Like a windstorm, Dominic Bash came into my life in the early spring of 1971. I was a mathematics graduate student at the University of Pennsylvania. Through his charm, wit, and persistence, Dominic nudged me into action. He said he was a homosexual, and foolishly, I believed that I had never met a homosexual in my entire life.

In my sheltered, conventional upbringing in Philadelphia, a very "Catholic" city, I heard the word "homosexual" only a few times and never with full understanding. Now this young man, with whom I conversed after a home liturgy, began to unfold the mystery of his life. He had entered a religious order but, after a short time, left that community because he believed that his homosexual orientation was incompatible with religious life. He was attending the Episcopal Church on campus because, as he said, the "Catholic Church doesn't want me."

His gay friends, cradle Catholics estranged from the Church that had shaped their values and religious convictions, longed to attend a Mass where their sexual orientation would not be an issue. A priest and I planned a welcoming Eucharist at Dominic's apartment. Like parched earth deluged with unremitting rains, Dominic and his friends soaked up the solace of that Mass. They reconnected with their Church, which had changed more than its liturgical language after the Second Vatican Council.

As Dominic's friends were amazed at the innovations they found in the Catholic Church, I too was amazed as my stereotypes of what it meant to be homosexual began to be challenged. At first, I thought that using the parish hall for monthly dances of the Gay Activist Alliance was like hosting a cocktail party for a group of alcoholics. I soon learned that, unlike alcoholism, homosexuality was not a disease. The psychiatric and psychological communities were having their own debates about this issue in the late 1960s and early '70s. In 1973, the American Psychiatric Association formally stated that homosexuality is not an emotional or mental disorder, and the following year the American Psychological Association issued a similar statement.

The change in my thinking about homosexuality came not from any professional associations but from personal experience. At a clergy conference on homosexuality sponsored by the Episcopal Church, I encountered a young woman who worked for the American Civil Liberties Union. She was intelligent and socially responsible, and had a healthy self-esteem. At the home liturgies I was organizing for Dominic and his friends, I met a librarian whose sense of commitment to his companion was a matchless model for all partnerships. I marveled at a lesbian mother who cared lovingly for her two children from a previous heterosexual marriage.

Because most of the homosexual people I encountered seemed as well balanced psychologically as the heterosexual people

I knew, I felt that society's labels of "unnatural" or "disordered" just did not fit. Except for the fact of their sexual orientation, my new friends seemed no different from my heterosexual ones. If being lesbian or gay was not a disease, then society had a responsibility to provide wholesome socializing experiences for gay and lesbian youth, adolescents, and adults. I never again compared gay dances to drinking parties for alcoholics.

I had never heard any leaders in my Church speak about homosexuality. Since any sexual activity outside a marriage for the express purpose of having children was considered immoral, according to traditional sexual ethics, I knew the religious judgment was a negative one. I never thought about this much, as I had little reason to, but when I did, I thought it was very unfair. To tell a lesbian or gay person that she or he must live a life alone, without a cherished partner to whom to express love, was simply not right.

After completing my graduate studies, I taught mathematics at the College of Notre Dame of Maryland. I always loved teaching, but my friendship with Dominic would ultimately alter the course of my life. His repeated question, "What is the Church doing for my gay brothers and sisters?" haunted me and my religious administrators.

I have had a fierce sense of justice since I was a young child. I remember standing up for one fifth-grade girl when others were trying to bully and ostracize her because of her background. This sense of social justice led to my attempts to rectify the injustices I heard in the stories of lesbian and gay people. The excitement, too, of learning about a new and fascinating area of life enticed me to leave formal teaching. Others were willing and able to teach mathematics, but there was no official Church ministry for lesbian and gay Catholics at that time. In 1977, my religious congregation, the School Sisters of Notre Dame, assigned me to full-time lesbian and gay ministry. Workshops, lectures, consultation, retreats, spiritual direction, writing, and research became my classroom. This was the beginning of the most significant education in my life.

Rejection and Criticism

I soon learned more. I learned that advocates of those who are ostracized often share the rejection and misunderstanding of the oppressed class. I think now of what Pope Francis said about those in ministry: shepherds must smell like the sheep.

I was popular among my Sisters and was elected for several sessions to the provincial assembly as the "young sister" delegate. As my Sisters began to hear of my involvement with the lesbian and gay community at the University, I could feel a shift in feeling, a subtle hesitancy, almost a fear of something considered taboo in those times. By the late 1970s I had co-founded, along with a Salvadorian priest, Fr. Robert Nugent, New Ways Ministry, a national Catholic organization to promote understanding and reconciliation between lesbian and gay Catholics and the wider Church. One Sister told me she liked the "old ways" better. I was not re-elected to the provincial assembly as a "young sister" delegate after my involvement with lesbian and gay Catholics became known. I believe there was a causal connection.

The Vatican

There was also a connection between my advocacy for lesbian and gay people and the censure I received from representatives of the institutional church. In 1988, the Congregation for Religious, the Vatican agency in charge of women religious, announced it was "studying" my ministry and set up a Vatican Commission. After three meetings with the Commission, my case was remanded to the Congregation for the Doctrine the Faith (CDF), formerly called "The Inquisition." My provincial leader, who was my immediate religious superior, was worried that I would be excommunicated. She felt we should make a pilgrimage to Munich to pray for a miracle at the tomb of our foundress. In the DaVinci Airport in Rome, we saw an elderly, white-haired man in a black clerical suit board the plane and sit five rows behind us. He looked familiar. I went back, sat down next to him, and began a conversation.

I learned that he was Cardinal Joseph Ratzinger, later known as Pope Benedict XVI, the head of the CDF, the Vatican agency now investigating me and my ministry.

When I told the Cardinal my name, I saw a slight twinkle in his blue eyes. "I have known you for twenty years," he said. In fact, he had collected several bulging files on me during those years. We talked about a number of things: how I got into the ministry, a document the U.S. bishops were writing for parents of lesbian and gay children, demonstrations by LGBT people, my reading his first book while I was in the novitiate, the decrease in the number of religious vocations. I doubt that the fifteen- to twenty-minute conversation changed the final decision of the CDF, but I believe that both Cardinal Ratzinger and I learned something from that encounter.

At least three times during our meeting, he whispered, "providence, providence." I believe he was seeing the hand of God in that chance encounter. My Superior General had asked Cardinal Ratzinger to meet with me to discuss the Vatican's concerns, but such a face-to-face meeting is not part of their process. Instead, the CDF follows a medieval process of appointing a theologian, unbeknown to the accused, to defend the accused in a secret meeting. I was informed that I had been accused, defended, and found guilty of error. I believe that Cardinal Ratzinger was thinking that the providence of God was working to bring us together.

Here was another learning moment for me in the significant education in my life. From that chance encounter with Cardinal Ratzinger, I was able to put a human face on the Church institution. I experienced the Cardinal's humanity; he was cordial, gentle, humorous, and personable. He was praying his breviary when I first sat down next to him, and as I left him, he said, "Pray for me, and I will pray for you." I believe each of us sensed that the other is deeply committed to the Church in the service of God's people. I learned that he and other Church leaders are caught in a medieval structure and do not know how to break out of it. The clerical system indoctrinated them in a worldview that is static, unbending, and bound by legalism. It knows nothing of the compassion and flexibility of Pope Francis's words, "Who am I to judge?" I have learned to pray for those who feel they need to follow such a straight and narrow road in ordering their own lives and the lives of others.

The Notification and Obediences

Despite my personal encounter with Cardinal Ratzinger on the plane, the investigation continued for another year, with inauspicious results. In 1999, Pope John Paul II approved a notification from the CDF that I was permanently prohibited from any pastoral work involving homosexual persons. For the next nine months I spoke to Catholic audiences about my dealings with the Vatican and reflected on my future in the quiet times of retreat.

Tens of thousands of letters arrived at the Vatican from all parts of the world, asking for a reconsideration of my case. Annoyed, the Vatican contacted my Superior General to remedy the situation. I was once again summoned to the community's headquarters in Rome and ordered not to speak or write about homosexuality or the processes leading to my censure, not to criticize the Vatican or the Bishops on sexual matters, and not to encourage the faithful to dissent from any official teachings.

As I sat in one of the offices, a vivid image came to mind. I saw the form of a woman who had been physically abused for years, battered by her domestic partner. I saw a wrinkled and sagging woman, made old beyond her years, who had remained silent because she was afraid. I saw a bent woman who feared further reprisals from the batterer. I saw a weeping woman concerned about the safety of her children if she spoke up.

I felt like that battered woman. I felt I was being intimidated to remain silent about the emotional abuse I had experienced. During the dozen years since the Vatican investigation was announced, I had been afraid to speak publicly because I was fearful of standing alone. I knew I would lose the support of my religious community leaders who were good women, whom I loved and respected, but who wanted to keep out of the public eye and show loyalty to the Vatican through their cooperation.

As I sat in that office, I learned that, in telling my story about the investigation to audiences the previous year, I had begun to lose my fear of what others thought of me. I had begun to experience the freedom that comes from finding one's voice and speaking one's story. Like the battered woman who mysteriously finds an inner fortitude to go to a shelter and begin to tell her story, and who gains more courage each time that story is recounted, I was given God's strength to respond: "I choose not to collaborate in my own oppression by restricting my basic human right to speak about my experience. To me this is a matter of conscience."

I felt an immense sense of freedom, despite the fact that soon after the meeting I sat in another room and sobbed uncontrollably. Hearing my weeping, my provincial leader came and embraced me in her big bear hug until the weeping eventually subsided. I was mourning the separation from the good women I had known and loved for forty years.

God Shoes

How could I take the bold step that would mean leaving the community I had lived and worked in for four decades? What enabled me to find this voice? A choice to set aside a directive from religious authorities and spiritual leaders that one respects doesn't feel comfortable. Why was I sure I was doing the right thing? I made many retreats and prayed fervently throughout the investigative process to discern God's path for me, but one retreat stands out in my mind.

During a retreat at a Carmelite Monastery, outside Baltimore, I walked briskly around the monastery grounds. I looked down at my sneakers and abruptly realized how well they fit my feet. I thought of my floppy Birkenstocks, which I usually wear, and knew I might trip with those Birkenstock sandals on my feet. I thought of the smart-looking shoes I often wore for more formal occasions. They would really hurt my feet after a sequence of jogs or long walks around the convent grounds. I certainly could walk in other shoes—shoes that were too big, too small, too loose, or too tight—for a *limited* time. But if I walked long enough in shoes that didn't fit, I would ruin my feet and, ultimately, my back, my posture, and my health.

That meditation on shoes became an allegory for me. The shoes that fit just right are the shoes that God asks me to walk in during life. Despite the fear of dismissal from my community, or even excommunication from the Church I loved, I needed to walk in the designer shoes that sported God's label. I had to walk in my "God shoes."

Why was I so *sure* that my calling, my God shoes, at this time was to continue to advocate for lesbian and gay people? Because I saw the unfairness of the Vatican process and the rightness of the lives of lesbian and gay people. That foundational sense of justice implanted in my being was the soles and arches of my God shoes.

I learned that "finding our God shoes" is a poetic way of saying that we need to engage in the process of making an informed decision of conscience. If we are to grow in our faith and our loving relationship with God, we must engage in moral discernment. Our God shoes require us to speak our truth, even if no one hears our voice, even if our speech is heard and opposed, even if we walk alone.

The Sisters of Loretto

My God shoes at this time in my life required me to speak my truth to my Superior General. She made it clear that if I did not obey I would receive two canonical warnings. If I persisted in resisting what was asked of me, the SSND General Council would vote on my dismissal from the community. I believe it was very difficult for these good women, who had supported this ministry for more than twenty years, to deliver repressive commands at the bidding of a patriarchal church.

Because I still felt called to religious life, and also to work for lesbian and gay persons, I considered transferring to another religious congregation that would embrace me and my ministry. Over the years I had worked with a number of Sisters of Loretto, who were all on fire with the justice and compassion of the Gospel. They were willing to speak truth to power and stood with the poor and oppressed. The Sisters of Loretto are a canonical congregation of women religious, founded in Kentucky in 1812 when Kentucky was the western frontier. As the United States moved westward, so did the Sisters of Loretto. They were, and still are, pioneer women.

I applied to transfer to the Sisters of Loretto and, after the three years of trial membership required by canon law, I made my final vow commitment at the Loretto Motherhouse. I feel very much at home in Loretto, as I believe the majority of members share my religious, political, and social views. I feel that I have wedded the SSND educational mission to the pioneering Loretto spirit.

Since my transfer into the Loretto Community, the Sisters of Loretto have received nine letters from the Vatican. The letters varied in wording, but the content was always the same: the Vatican objected to my involvement in LGBT ministry, called upon the Loretto president to enforce the Vatican Notification, and urged dismissal proceedings if I persisted in LGBT ministry.

The Loretto president responded cordially, sometimes firmly, to the letters, indicating that I was doing the justice work the Community was called to do. Loretto has not heard from the Vatican since 2009, the very year that the Vatican announced a visitation of all U.S. apostolic religious communities and a doctrinal assessment of the Leadership Conference of Women Religious (LCWR). Both the visitation of the religious communities and the doctrinal assessment of LCWR concluded favorably for the Sisters in 2015. In my own case, I received VIP treatment at the Vatican in response to my letter to Pope Francis about the pilgrimage I was leading for LGBT Catholics and their families and friends. When our pilgrims arrived at St. Peter's Square for the general audience with Pope Francis on Ash Wednesday 2015, a papal usher led me and the fifty pilgrims past the thousands of people in the square to the top platform in front of the high doors of the basilica where Pope Francis would be sitting to address the crowd. Pope Francis is setting a new and welcome tone from the Vatican for Sisters and for LGBT people.

Additional Insights

Over the course of more than forty years as an advocate in my Church for LGBT people, I have gained many insights. I learned that no mission can be achieved without the support of many people. I have been able to engage in LGBT ministry because others stand there with me. Despite the opposition of those who fear or who do not understand, I have been able to remain faithful because of support from the School Sisters of Notre Dame, the Sisters of Loretto, and many others too numerous to name.

I learned that ecclesiastical structures need to change. Church leaders need to practice the principle of subsidiarity called for by the Second Vatican Council. Subsidiarity means that matters should be handled at the local level when possible, not by the most centralized authority. In my case, the Vatican asked the School Sisters of Notre Dame to evaluate my ministry on three separate occasions, and the Vatican should have accepted the positive evaluations that were given. For the principle of subsidiarity to work, the higher body should not take matters into its own hands just because they believe the "right" decision was not made.

I learned that the years of investigation provided a good case study for an analysis of ecclesiastical power. Obedience is used as a tool to force people to bend to the wishes of those with authority. Those in power are often not interested in a discussion of persons' lives or what effect their opinions have on others. Those in power want only to make others bend to their will, claiming it is God's will. But God's will for each of us is to find our God shoes, to follow our conscience, no matter how difficult it may be. Walking in one's God shoes may require ecclesiastical disobedience. The past has taught me that legitimate dissent and nonviolent resistance to unjust laws can lead to the development of Church doctrine. The change in the teaching on slavery is a prime example. Individuals and groups condemned the institution of slavery, and countries instituted laws to protect human beings from being treated as mere property. By the end of the nineteenth century the Vatican finally acknowledged that the voices raised in opposition to the tradition of slavery had merit and declared that slavery was inherently evil. Similarly, by following one's conscience and publicly dissenting from the status quo, a person can contribute to how the Holy Spirit may be leading the Church. Each of us has a role to play in enabling the whole community to arrive at the truth.

A host of issues and principles related to this case merit further analysis. These include identifying the central teachings of the Church on homosexuality and sexuality, noting the negative effects of the Vatican on lesbian and gay persons and their families, developing educational and pastoral initiatives to welcome LGBT persons into all facets of Church life, limiting interference in the internal affairs of a religious congregation, ascertaining the advantages and disadvantages of canonical status for religious congregations, recognizing the role of a public minister, stabilizing the fragility of human rights in the Church, and setting up fair and just procedures and penalties in ecclesiastical disputes. I leave these issues for future discussion.

I myself have learned more than enough for one lifetime from my more than forty years of ministry. For now, I pray only for the wisdom to follow my conscience, to know when to bend and when to stand firm, and to recognize which pair of God shoes to wear at any given time. For Church leadership, I pray for the freedom and courage to take risks. For LGBT Catholics and their families, I pray for the healing of anger and hurt and for their full inclusion in the Church. For the People of God, I pray for an infusion of the Spirit of Vatican II. As I pray for all these people, I repeat one of my favorite quotations from scripture, from St. Paul: "For those who love God, all things work together unto good" (Romans 8:28).

She, with the Alabaster Jar

Victoria Marie

In Matthew and John and Mark
　　the Twelve scold her about purse strings.
In Luke, the Pharisee remarks
　　she's a sinner, a cursed thing.

To all Jesus responds, "She understands
　　what is to come and responds in a loving way.
You act outwardly as propriety demands.
Your inward thoughts are cause for dismay."

Down through the ages, she'll be recalled,
　　though they try to smear and defame her.
What she has done will be remembered by all,
　　though they try to diminish and un-name her.

What does it mean for women today?
We remained at the foot of the cross and
　　Jesus chose women by whom to be anointed.
For these things, they want to make us pay.
They want to show us who is the boss,
But it was the Magdalene Jesus first appointed.

Just like Mary Magdalene, we have been sent
   to spread the Word regardless of official consent,
   with the fire of love in our hearts to give, unsparing,
   to bring love to the world by serving and caring,
   at home, at work, in ceremony, in preaching.
Spread love and good news! That's Jesus' teaching.

The Chancery

Jean Molesky-Poz

On July 27, 1976, I composed one of the most important letters of my life. Addressed to Pope Paul VI, my letter asked him to free me from the perpetual vows I had made just one year before, solemnly sworn promises to live in obedience, poverty, and consecrated virginity for the rest of my life. If the Vatican granted my request, I would no longer be a nun.

Such written letters follow an ecclesial formula, structured by canon law in which the Church's authority is vested in the Pope as the supreme lawgiver. I addressed it "Your Holiness," and identified myself as a perpetually professed member of the Sisters of St. Francis. I explained my reasons:

- I have reached a new level of self-understanding and need to take on a new responsibility for my life— that is, my experience of God has changed from a parent-child relationship to understanding myself as a woman: responsible, creative, and able to make decisions;

- I have a new awareness of the integration of spirituality and sexuality;

- My concept of community has evolved from the traditional model of religious life to one embracing various cultures and lifestyles.

"It is not that I cannot continue to grow within this community," I wrote, "but I believe that I can be further challenged to grow in a fuller way outside of the community." I told the Holy Father I felt as sure of this "call" to re-enter the world as I did of my decision to enter the Franciscan community eleven years earlier.

I had to tell the Pope that this had not been a quick or solitary decision, and that it had been made with discernment. In religious life, great value is placed on the process of coming to understand how God is working in one's life. The process of discernment helps one perceive the different movements that are produced within oneself.

At such times, one is faced with large questions: What is of God? What is of other spirits? Are there forces moving within me that work against God? One works to overcome deluding oneself. When one takes on a spiritual life, subtle forces subvert you. In this practice, a person listens as clearly as possible to one's intuition, heart, and mind within the context of prayer for God's movement in one's life. It is meant to be a journey of seeing, understanding, making a judgment, and acting on that judgment. What assures discernment is that God speaks to us in peace.

From our first days in religious life, Sister José, our postulant director, trained us to "examine our conscience" fifteen minutes both at noon and at night. Once a month, we each met with a spiritual director to discuss the promptings of our lives. The process advanced into high gear every year when we made an eight-day retreat in total silence. In those often long days and nights, I had learned that discerning promptings from God is not straightforward—many voices compete for our attention, and these spiritual voices are quite subtle. Since I was making this life-changing decision, only a year and a half after professing my final vows, I knew it was critical that I understood accurately from what spirit the impulses of my soul emanated.

The Pope had to know I had discerned this call with the help of others: the Director of the Franciscan congregation and a member of her Council, my spiritual director of five years, and two other priests, one of whom was a clinical psychologist. I wrote to the Pope that I had also consulted with several Franciscan women and with lay Catholics. I weighed my words carefully. I ended the letter with the formal request: "I humbly beg Your Holiness to grant me the dispensation from my vows."

On September 17, two months after writing my letter to the Pope, I sat in an armchair in the gray linoleum foyer of the Diocese of Oakland Roman Catholic chancery office. I pulled the note out of my purse to make sure I had the right time. I had waited twenty minutes, which was unusual, as most Church functions begin promptly. I felt anxious, an anxiety born not of doubt but of the irrevocability of the act I was about to commit.

Heavy steps sounded up the stairs, and a bald man dressed in a full-length robe came into the lobby. I knew from his clothing how I should address him. I would have known any time in the last six hundred years. He wore an impeccably tailored black Roman-style cassock, detailed with a row of tiny red silk buttons running from neck to foot. Red piping trimmed his collar, running down the front placket and around the hem; a wide magenta band cincture bound his ample waist, its silk-fringed sash cascading down the front.

I may as well have been hurtled back into fourteenth-century France, when the Pope lived in Avignon. Priests working in papal offices were clothed just this way and addressed as "mon seigneur"—"my lord." Here I was face to face with a symbol of a medieval church structure.

"Hello, Monsignor," I said, extending my hand. "I've come to sign the papers."

"Oh, yes, Sister," he said, glancing at my sandals, paisley skirt, and loose beige blouse. It was a cool look that I could not read. "Your papers have arrived from the Vatican."

We approached a glassed-in counter under a sign: Office of Canon Law. He rapped with his knuckle at the receptionist who sat behind security glass. She was dressed in a well-tailored navy blue suit. She set aside papers and slid the glass window open.

"Carmen, may I have the papers for Sister?"

"Yes, Most Reverend."

The wire-meshed glass sent me in a spin. It reminded me of a prison or asylum. What needed to be kept under lock and key? Was there something I didn't know about the Roman Catholic Church?

I felt my face flush, my hands go clammy. I didn't doubt my decision, but at this moment my private struggle suddenly had become a public and official event, tied to church law.

The monsignor flipped through the Vatican papers. "I need two witnesses," he said to the receptionist.

She nodded politely. Hearing the sound of someone walking into the lobby, the monsignor swirled around.

"Do you have a minute, Father?" he said, stopping a priest. He was young and wore a clerical black suit and white Roman collar.

That small-notched clerical collar, or *collarino*, dating back to the seventeenth century, marked a priest as available to perform the sacraments even if he wasn't dressed in vestments. It meant you could spot a priest and flag one down if someone was dying. Well, I wasn't dying, but he was definitely flagged down.

"Can you be a witness for the dispensation of final vows?" the monsignor asked.

"Surely, Most Reverend," the smooth-faced priest said, nodding to the monsignor. He politely recognized me.

I felt uncomfortable. I just wanted to get out of there.

The monsignor dug into the fold of his magenta cincture and pulled out a white handkerchief. He used it discreetly, then slipped it back again. His hazel eyes swept over us quickly. "I think we are ready to begin," he said.

This was it? I had never, ever imagined ending eleven years of religious life with three strangers in front of a panel of security glass and in such a bureaucratic manner. But it seemed to me that for the monsignor this was a rote activity, like stamping baptismal or death certificates.

With secretary and priest standing close by, the monsignor set the papers on the counter ledge and handed me a fountain pen. He pulled up his red-piped cuff and, pointing to the dotted line, held the documents steady. I bent over and tried to read line by line, but my heart pounded so I could hardly concentrate. Besides, they were in Latin. I could not summon my four years of high school Latin to clear meanings.

What were these three strangers thinking? I wanted them to know how I was not choosing less, but more. I wanted them to know I was committing to my faith not within safe institutional walls, but among ordinary people, creating history yet still fastened to the contemplative anchor. But now was not the time for this explanation. My knees felt weak. It will be over in a few minutes, I told myself.

Slowly and deliberately I twisted the cap off the fountain pen, then pressed the nib against the linen parchment. I signed my name confidently and quickly across the line. I saw the black ink bleed and become part of the Vatican document. The witnesses signed their names. The secretary handed the monsignor a blotter to seal the wet ink.

Examining the document, the monsignor said, "Now, I think that's it."

As quickly and dryly as this signing was begun, it was ended.

He excused the witnesses and we were alone again. Looking into the manila envelope, the monsignor said to me, "Oh, wait a minute, I think there's a check for you."

I figured the money, something like a severance pay "to get me started," would be about $2000. I had taught high school for five years, and Dad had made many financial contributions to the community. Dad also had paid the humble dowry of $50 when I entered.

"Make sure there's a check in there," the monsignor said.

I opened the envelope. The check was for $639.18.

"It's here, yes," I said. Who decided this amount? But then, I had lived a vow of poverty; what did I expect? What about my years of teaching? I couldn't solve this now.

"Sister," the monsignor said, placing his hand on my shoulder, "if there is anything we can do for you, just let us know." Was he being sincere, or patronizing? What could I really ask of him? What could he offer me? And who was the "we"?

I thanked him, walked down the stairs, pushed open the glass door to the open air, and burst into tears.

Next door to the chancery office was a church. I turned and chased up the cement steps, and slipped into the back pew. The building was empty and dark. I dropped my head into my open hands and sobbed.

In ten minutes, the dispensation was all over. Not even a word of thanks from the monsignor. He represented the Church. I had given eleven years, perhaps the best of my young life, to serve the Church. Dismissed. I was dismissed, just dismissed. Treated as a piece of ecclesial structure.

Several people have asked if I felt I should have apologized to the monsignor, as symbol of the Church, for not following through on my religious vows. After all, I volunteered to go; no one came knocking at my front door to recruit me. I'm the one who sensed the call to religious life. But an apology never occurred to me, and still doesn't. I so needed to guard my inner core from the medieval institution to which I had handed my life. That day, and for many months, I felt fragile, but sure.

For the secretary, priest, and monsignor, it had been a bureaucratic procedure, but for me, it closed the door on convent life. They didn't know how much I loved the community, that I felt called to something more, a more contemplative life, and that I wanted to live the Gospel without all the safeguards of the institution.

Now, as I write, I wonder how the witnesses felt. Did they see me as losing my faith? Abandoning them? Not being able to persevere? Taking the lower road? Or did they begin to see a crack in the medieval structures of religious life?

I was surely not the first to sign such papers in the chancery office. In fact, by the late 1970s the number of women requesting dispensations was so great that the only way Church officials could handle them was through bureaucratic numbness. After Vatican

II, in the late 1960s through the early 1980s, 60,000, or 31 percent, of women religious left the convent. They call it "the mass exodus."

In time, I quieted myself. The flame in the red tabernacle lamp showed in the sanctuary, steadying my heart.

There in the dark church, I prayed:

Dear God, I am so grateful for all you have given me: my family, my education, and these years in religious life, a time to know and love you deeply and dearly. But I know you call me to a bigger world, beyond the security of the institution, to build a community that includes many different peoples, not just celibate women. Please show me how I can use my talents for others, for farm workers, for immigrants, for the poor. I have seen many women and men struggle not for themselves but for others. I have seen farm workers endure hunger, fasts, boycotts, and marches to demand fair laws. They are the face of the suffering Church I have come to love. Show me how I can throw in my lot with them. I entrust my life into your hands. Show me your way.

Yet the Romanesque-style church building gave no solace. Its thick, heavy, concrete and reddish-brown Italian marble walls created a cavernous interior, and because the noon sun was overhead, no light streamed through the stained-glass windows. Their figures were mere leaded panes of muted purple and gray geometric shapes, casting a pallid, cold hue. I knew God was everywhere, but I doubted that God, or my sense of the Mystery of God, could feel welcomed in this vault.

I walked out into the bright light, crossed the street, and sat on the shore of Lake Merritt, an urban park in Oakland. I listened to picnickers laughing and watched joggers running around the lake. A father and son tossed pebbles into the lake; ducks paddled. The autumn air warmed my face. I thought, yes, my life belongs out here among ordinary people.

No One Has Hired Us

Ann Breslin

Triangles, always triangles. Somehow when I doodled, through boredom or daydreaming, those doodles always came out as triangles. Was it something primordial? Something to do with being Irish, being imbued with the shamrock and St. Patrick's breastplate—"I bind unto myself today the strong name of the Trinity"—or was it just coincidence?

Growing up during the "Troubles" I didn't have much interest in religion. The traditional family rosary, sporadically followed, bored me. Sunday Mass was no better. Counting the number of windows in the local chapel kept me entertained. As I reached my early teens my mother began to go to daily Mass, and my younger sister went with her. Eventually I began to tag along too. I was an early-morning person, anyway. Once at the chapel, I still counted the windows . . . but gradually, so slowly I didn't realize it was happening, the stories began to hook me.

It is a cliché, but the world was dark, dreary, and damp. The annual Retreat, or "Mission" as the rural people called it, was a relief. For the first week, we women were all together early in the morning and again in the evening. Then, for the second week, it was the men's turn. All men out of the house for seven evenings in a trot. Space in the house, choice in what to watch on television, the women together without the men—bliss!

Well, that was the theory (or the theology). But somehow the men's Mission could be curtailed to accommodate the football game in a way that the women's was never shortened or made easier for anything—not for a sick child, an aging parent, an exciting episode of the local soap opera. I felt a burning sense of injustice, an unfair double standard.

The world was too male for me: at home, a strict and dominant father and a crowd of brothers; outside, armed soldiers leering and shouting abuse. My feelings were conflicted by the death of my mother's only brother—my uncle, a soldier—dying in France before he was twenty-one.

One morning after the retreat Mass, going up Chapel Lane toward the shops to fetch the bread we really liked to break, the still warm baps that all the women in the family shared at breakfast. As I was walking toward the bakery, I spotted a gunman on the roof, flat but alert, rifle at the ready, a line from me to him. Following his concentrated look, I saw what engaged his attention: across Bishop's field two army jeeps were driving slowly along the road, a soldier popping out of each.

My sight line to the gunman, his to the soldiers, the soldiers back to me.

Below the gunman, a line of women just out from Mass were waiting for hot baps, doughnuts, turnovers, scones. Their space and sharing was about to be invaded by self-appointed heroes, the ones who had burned my playmates to death in the name of freedom and their counterparts, patrolling, controlling. Not for the first time, I pondered the futility of replacing one elite with another—they all looked the same to me: white and male. The lives of women didn't improve; violence wasn't the answer.

I wanted a way beyond politics, beyond the family. I wanted a different life.

Could there be a different way?

The convent was different. Independent women, questioning, challenging . . . conforming.

Images and memories float up and disappear again:

The priest celebrating Eucharist but having breakfast served in a special room after the convent Mass, a Sister delegated to keep him company.

The glass of brandy poured for the visiting priest but never in celebration of one of the Sisters.

The man of the road, in the back hall with the cracked mug, the tax-avoiding business man in the dining room with the best china.

The endless service: the priest wearing the dress but the nuns doing the serving.

Once at Easter in the cathedral, having convinced a small group, including a curate, to have a para-liturgy, our preparations were interrupted by the Bishop's secretary, unhappy at having a woman (me) standing on the sanctuary.

I stood beside him and asked him to look down the cathedral and describe what he saw: he saw the stained-glass windows; he saw the organ in the choir loft; he saw the great wooden doors; he saw the Stations of the Cross.

I asked what prevented him from seeing, from hearing, the women, only women, vacuuming the carpet, brushing and washing the floor, polishing the pews. What prevented him from seeing the women washing where, the next day, Maundy Thursday, by decree of the Bishop, only men would have their feet pretend to be washed?

The sexism of my family made me a feminist. The sexism of the Church made me a feminist.

Have you ever noticed how the symbol for church ♁ is that for a woman, turned upside down? ♀

The Bishop didn't like my profession ceremony. The Bishop wanted to veto some of the prayers because they referred to Deborah and Ruth, or maybe because they referred to the women's strength and courage, to their standing upright.

"They want the trappings, you want the marrow," an elderly retreat director told me once. "You'll be hurt." And I was.

Without ever once speaking directly to me, they removed me from the Vocations Council. I may have been young, but I was too challenging to be useful.

They removed me from the youth group; perhaps my talks were more inspiring than theirs, but the rumored reason was the Bishop wanted only a priest to act as spiritual director.

And when I removed myself from them, they annulled my thirteen years of commitment in just a few weeks. Even my mother said, "They must have been glad to get rid of you."

In place of me and others like me, they kept a pedophile.

In place of me and others like me, they kept a man having a series of affairs.

In place of me and others like me, they kept a man who could watch a woman being beaten in the street and not intervene.

These men they called priests. These men others called Father.

Many years later, I met the one who had me removed from the Vocations Council. The scandal of the sexual abuse of children had broken; there were inquiries and judge-led reports.

"We need more ♀ in the ♁," he said, without irony, with breathtaking sincerity.

Pain Cries to a Patriarchal Church

Mary Ellen Rufft

The Altered Boy

I'd just turned nine.
He said he liked me best
Of all the other altar boys.
We wrestled each other
Like the guys do on TV,
With only our shorts on.
It felt strange that first time,
His touch, different from the others.
I knew he liked me best
Of all the other altar boys.
I'm eleven now.
He went away last month.
"A big cheese" dad says,
In charge of boys becoming priests
Like him.

I miss him lots, but no one knows.
I think he liked me best
Of all the other altar boys.

A Pillar of Power

He was my father,
Yet fathered me never.
My mother, dead when I was five,
Loved me in my dreams.
Her husband taught me with his body
How power crushes,
How lust burns,
How torture weakens.
I understood none of what he did
And little of what he said.
Foreign remained his words to me
At six, and eight, and twelve.
At fourteen, they became flesh
Within me.
I feared his wrath, the stares,
The pain.
I had my insides cleansed of him
And learned
What excommunication means.
He pillars still our parish Church.

Only a Stone

Nine children ours—
In as many years.
The rhythm of our love
Made all times fertile.
Unemployed now and sad.
He strains for signs of hope.
Your "thou shalt not"
To me is like the stone
You would not have
A mother give for bread.

Crooked Since Birth

I knew when only five,
But called myself a liar for years.
I prayed to be like you, or you,
Ordinary, normal, acceptable.
No hope in surgery nor therapy.
Neither drugs nor bloodied wrists
Brought light to my mother's eyes,
Nor forgiveness from your lips.
I beg you, Father, miracle me,
As Jesus did of old.
Say to me: "Arise. Be made straight."
Or, if you cannot,
Say, at least, "Go in peace,
Your faith has saved you."

Twice Broken Vows

A nightmare honeymoon
Introduced me to conjugal "bliss."
No longer courtship gentleness,
No more a lover's caress.
Now only broken bones,
Bruising hurts,
Bleeding cuts.
Yesterday's unhealed wounds,
Re-opened by husbandly fist.
Four boys, two girls, five broken bones.
Twenty-two years as "helpmate."
And you tell me still
I should have stayed
Because I promised.

Bed or Bread?

An "A" you print
Upon my breast
And cross the street,
Lest my presence
Taint your well-groomed soul.
You speak truth of me.
Too weak I am
To watch my children
Beg for bread
And choose instead
To sell my body
Cheap at any price.
You say to me
I sin for both
Each time I lure man,
The image made like God,
Into my bed.
Yet why no words of blame
To husband or to pimp,
One soused on booze,
The other drunk with power?

Most of the speakers in "Pain Cries" are composites of people I've counseled in my private psychology practice. I've been blessed to see many of them move through their pain to attain inner peace and a resurrected spirit. The following poem, "A Resurrection," describes a little of one woman's journey.

A Resurrection

Pieces of her story
Came tumbling out.
Then,
For a time,
Almost nothing.
Afraid she'd said too much,
Her face mirrored her questions.
"Would I believe her?
Was it wrong to tell all about my dad?
And what his friends did too?"

Meanwhile, I listened,
Put on her shoes,
Imagined what she'd endured.
Listened until her pain
Became, almost, my own.

She saw that I believed
And cared
Perhaps even understood,
Allowed herself to cry then
Sad, quiet tears
For weeks.

A less gentle flow came later
Anger began to rage
She beat the pillows,
Tore up old phone books,
Screamed curse words
In her car.
Cried gut-wrenching sobs.
Walked miles
Mumbling encouraging mantras

Years later,
We could pray together
For her peace,
Talk about God being with her
Even back then,
Share the faith and hope
That had transformed her heart.
She called her journey
From despair to hope
A resurrection.
I think of it as grace.

Part Two

Our Mother Works

Sister Dorothy Stang, Assassinated

Liz Dolan

She went to Anapu, Para, forty years ago to teach
the dirt-poor peasants: manioc, first; cocoa,

then coffee and peppers. They called her Madre Mae.
Rose rings of light sank through the umbrella-canopy,

as rain ran off the drip spouts of leaves soiled by filth
she could not clean. It was Lincoln's birthday.

Now she decays like leaf litter, her nutrients weaving
into the understory of the forest; the lianas vine

about her ankles, bromeliads and periwinkle grace
her requiem. She should have feared the horns in the bushes,

the flat white face of death. Blood speckles
the rain forest floor; bullets berry-stain her best blouse.

Unruly Women: Nuns Out of Order

Carole Ganim

All of my life, I have lived in metaphor. From childhood to nun-hood to personhood, I have been captive to imagination and poetry, to story and song. Major metaphors have shaped my life in sig-nificant ways at significant times. I grew up in the safe, Catholic, middle-class world of Ohio in the middle of the twentieth century and entered the convent wishing fervently to give my life to God and to be a holy woman, as the vocabulary and context of my life at that time understood it. I prayed and dreamt of the romance of love of Jesus, never using the obnoxious metaphor of the Bride of Christ, yet somehow believing that I was engaged in a sacred relationship. I took vows that were the foundation of my life, yet, inevitably, I saw that they too were metaphorical representations of bondage and promise. I became an English professor, studying the literature of the great writers and seeing that the basis of any great art is metaphor, the ability to look at one thing and see something else or to describe the world as a shadow of reality, not the reality itself. I understood that language is symbol, that symbol can approach reality, but is not reality. Then I comprehended that reality is only an artifact of the mind anyway. So I have come full circle, accepting metaphor as one of the basic constructs of mind and imagination.

Here I want to discuss the role of former nuns from my perspective and that of others whom I have interviewed formally and informally as nuns who were out of order, actually and metaphorically. We were, and often are still, living lives out of order, *unruly*, if you will, that is, living not according to the rules. Like children, who accept the givens of their lives until and unless they know better, most of us just accepted the state of women religious as eternally designated by God and practiced by the Church from the beginning. Somewhere along the way, we began to know better. My discussion here locates our experiences within the framework of several essential life-defining metaphors. In particular, I will look at the metaphors of the journey, "the great No," and being out of order.

Looking out my window, I see the wind rustling the leaves of the great trees there. I have often paused while writing to contemplate these trees, these majestic witnesses of life, but the branches of one of the oldest trees are gnarled, and its trunk's skin is broken and leathery like the skin of old people. It is shedding its yellowed leaves early because it cannot sustain their weight anymore. I love the metaphor of the tree, the tree of life, and I love the beauty of the tree, any tree. The shape of the tree grounded in the earth, growing high, spreading branches, reaching toward the sun, dressing itself in various shades of green, producing leaves and fruit—the sheer beauty of the tree has always entranced me. But now one of my favorite trees is dying. This too is truth and metaphor.

The Journey

Certainly, the journey is the basic metaphor of life and literature. Life has a beginning, a middle, and an end. Always. It is so obvious that even Aristotle said that unity of action in drama demands a plot with a beginning, a middle, and an end. Life is also a plot with a beginning, middle, and end. Art imitates life, does it not? Or is it the other way around? We all start at birth on our journey, do some things along the course of that journey, and end it at some point. The poets and artists tell that story over and over again with a myriad of variations but always the same basic metaphor. So the Greeks trudged off to Troy to battle and then returned home; so Odysseus wended his way home for ten years; so Aeneas went across the sea to found Rome; so Dante came to the Inferno; so Arthur sought the Holy Grail. All the great stories and the lesser as well tell about the journey of life in some way or another. The story of women who entered the convent and then left is another journey story that has been told many times and in many different ways, but it is always about a journey. The speaker in Mary Oliver's poem "The Journey" hears voices shouting at her to mend her life, and she sets out on a journey because "you knew what you had to do" (13) and keeps going until she leaves the voices behind:

> And there was a new voice
> which you slowly
> recognized as your own,
> that kept you company
> as you strode deeper and deeper
> into the world
> determined to do
> the only thing you could do—
> determined to save
> the only life you could save. (27–36)

All of us who left the convent can relate to this poem because it presents the journey of claiming one's self; certainly we recognize the agony of rejecting voices "shouting/their bad advice" (4–5) and making the house tremble. We can relate to stumbling over branches and stones late at night until finally the stars "began to burn/through the sheets of clouds" (25–26). The metaphor fits. The journey is our story, the story of nuns who were on a fixed path, but had to leave it because of some inner and outer voices. It is the story of innumerable women and men who found that they must keep going on their journey, like the aged Ulysses in Tennyson's poem who must "sail beyond the sunset, and the baths/ Of all the western stars, until I die" (60–61). The metaphor has a million configurations, all iterating the great metaphor of life, the journey. Think of all the sub-mets: lost my way; off the beaten path; on the right road; off track; turning a corner; heading in the right (or wrong) direction; the detour; the road to success; dead end; roadblock; the way to hell is . . . ; the light at the end of the tunnel; the bridge over troubled waters; and so on.

When I was a novice, I wrote *To That Call,* a choric poem that our novitiate performed for the whole congregation. It was the story of our journey thus far, our entry into religious life and our intentions and wishes to continue along its path. We spoke the lines as if in a chorus, to the accompaniment of Wagner's *Overture to Lohengrin.* I see us now, a group of earnest, spiritual young things hoping what we were saying was true, convinced then that it was.

> Religion is a long, long road,
> A traveled route that each must go alone,
> A sacred way, an honored course,
> But new and strange at first,
> New and difficult to us fresh from the world,
> Still toddling in the inexperience of youth,
> Still gazing at the stars, oblivious of the pebbles. (36–42)

We were caught up in the metaphor of journeying to God, working through the brambles of life, remaining steadfast along the road, arriving at union with God. It was real and intentional. We were unaware of the experiences that were to come later, as they do to every person, where we would be in the "dusky wood" with Dante as he came to the Inferno:

> Midway upon the journey of our life
> I found that I was in a dusky wood;
> For the right path, whence I had strayed, was lost.
>   (*Inferno, Canto 1*: 1–3)

The people who journey thus are often the renegades who cannot fit into an ordered society; sometimes they are the visionaries who cannot fit nicely into a set form. Sometimes these people are scorned; at other times they are admired. Sometimes it takes a long time for others to admit that the ones who left the worn path were right. In other ways, the worn path is stable and tried, a testament to perseverance and fortitude, as in Eudora Welty's story "The Worn Path." Phoenix Jackson, from "far out in the country" walked on the worn path to town to get medicine for her grandson "as regular as clockwork" (1360, 1364). It wasn't an easy path, but she kept going. "She walked on. The shadows hung from the oak trees to the road like curtains" (1363).

We former nuns see ourselves as prophets, as those who could see what was coming in culture and church and the role of women. Sometimes we were just rebellious or recalcitrant, but I believe that the vast majority of us left our communities because we had to as a matter of conscience. We liked the worn path, but we had to take another road. Our journey has been neither easier nor harder than it would have been had we stayed on our path, but it has been our journey of choice.

The Great "No"

As I began questioning my chosen life, I read a poem by Constantine Cavafy, the great Alexandrian Greek poet, called "Che Fece . . . Il Gran Rifiuto," or "The Great No."

> To certain people there comes a day
> when they must say the great Yes or the great No.
> He who has the Yes ready within him
> Reveals himself at once, and saying it he crosses over
> to the path of honor and his own conviction.
> He who refuses does not repent. Should he be asked
>   again,
> He would say No again. And yet that No—
> The right No—crushes him for the rest of his life.

Cavafy's poem was inspired by a line from the *Inferno* referring to Pope Celestine's abdication from the papacy in 1294. Dante saw the abdication as an act of cowardice, ". . . the shade of him/ Who basely made the great renunciation" (*Inferno, Canto* 3:52–53), but Cavafy admired Celestine as a man of conscience who knew he was not temperamentally suited to the role of Pope and felt he could not perform the duties required.

"Che Fece . . . Il Gran Rifiuto" became the great metaphor about decision and conscience to me. I knew that I was facing a crucial moment in my life when I must be honest with myself about who I was and what I wanted. To refuse a life I had freely accepted and loved was at times an incomprehensible step, but I kept feeling the voice within me, and eventually I had to cross over to what I believed was the "path of honor and . . . conviction." The great yes and the great no were portals I had to choose between. I finally said yes to conscience.

The hardest task after making that decision was trying to explain it to my community, family, and friends. I often did poorly at that task, eventually settling into a formulaic answer of a few mumbled phrases. Occasionally I was able to articulate my reasons to some people, reasons that had to do with the changes within the world and the feeling that there was more to life than arguing about rules and regulations within religious communities and propping up the patriarchal and hierarchical nature of the Church. I acknowledged that with my *No.* I was leaving a good life of dedication and service and that I had deep regrets, but I was looking toward a bigger world with my *Yes.*

I carried a copy of "Che Fece . . . Il Gran Rifiuto" with me for many years as a metaphorical reminder of my big decision, but also as a support when I had other decisions to make. My book of Cavafy poems still occupies an important place on my bookshelf.

Out of Order

Being Out of Order is the title of the book I wrote (Vandamere Press, 2013) about my generation of Catholic nuns who entered the convent in the mid-twentieth century and left in large numbers several decades later. We were and are prophets who understood early on what the changes in the world would generate within religious life.

We were literally out of order, we nuns who left our religious communities. We had leapt over the walls, as did Monica Baldwin in 1941 when she left her cloistered community. She later wrote her autobiography, *I Leap Over the Wall* (1950). We had no physical walls, but we did leave the order.

Yes, we were literally out of order when we left our communities and our vows, but we were also metaphorically out of order. We met one of the definitions of *out of order* in the *Oxford English Dictionary*: "in breech of the rules of an organization." We were in breech, not so much of the day-to-day rules, but in breech of the rules we made vows to keep: poverty, chastity, and obedience, the larger order. We began to realize that the larger import of the vows was demeaning to us as women and as Christians. To be out of order meant that we were leaving the construct of a life defined by order so that we might more fully engage in a world of insecurity, disorder, even chaos. We were, in a sense, choosing a freer, riskier way of life, one not so circumscribed by the rule and the order, but by choice and freedom. The traditional vows, though lofty in spiritual intent, no longer served us in our contemporary world. They were, in many ways, worn-out metaphors of another time.

Poverty was a noble ideal, a way to say to the world that simplicity of life and detachment from material ambition and possession was to imitate Jesus more closely and to love one's fellow beings more sincerely. Francis of Assisi was the model here. We were not asked to tear off our clothes and run about preaching, but we were asked to have little and to be content with little. This we did well, I believe, but, in fact, we were never really poor. We never had to worry about where we would sleep, what we would eat, how we would pay our bills, what we would wear. We had security; we were not poor as the poor really are. Because we never suffered the anxiety and deprivation of the poor, we really did not understand what it meant to be poor, so our vow was virtual, metaphorical, not real. This, in turn, led us in some cases to not understand the poor, the fact of poverty, the reality of not having a place to lay one's head. It led to our not opening our convent doors to an indigent man because he was dirty or the addicted woman because she had asked once too often for help. We were often more committed to our rule and our order than to the untimely or irritating needs of the poor at our door because they disrupted the neat order of our lives. When we chose to go out of order, some of us became part of the unruly poor at the doorsteps of the secure, and others of us devoted our energies to going beyond the order of convent, city, school, or town to learn about and respond to the realities of poverty in our culture and the needs of the poor. I think this was an excellent reason to be out of order. If one understands what poverty really is, a vow to practice poverty is not enough; one must demand justice as well. Justice says that everyone should have the security of a person who need not worry about the essentials of life. One should not take a vow of poverty and obey the rule of the house to maintain order; one should insist upon and work for justice for the individual and collective poor.

Chastity as a religious vow also was based on noble ideals. We vowed chastity to free ourselves from deep human attachments so we might be dedicated to God. We left our homes and our family in order to live a more perfect life, to enter into the "State of Perfection" and to serve people in the name of Jesus. Certainly, this kind of dedication was praiseworthy, and in many ways it did allow more freedom to serve others. The downfall, however, of such a vow was that it effectively denied our humanity. Chastity denied not only sexuality but also all the relationships that demand a personal, affectional commitment of one person to another. This often resulted in distance from emotion and attachment to self. Some of us were self-absorbed, cold, uncaring. Others were just dried up like Langston Hughes's "raisin in the sun." As Chastity became spiritualized as a vow rejecting one's sinful flesh in order to be purified, the vow also became an instrument of control of women within the Church.

Those of us who chose to become officially out of order could no longer accept the ancient assumptions of male superiority sanctioned within the Church and our own communities. Neither could we accept the belief that chastity was intrinsically more virtuous than a physical, sexual, and emotional life, as we had witnessed conclusive evidence of the opposite. We saw all of the vows as means of sustaining the power structure, and we wanted no part of it.

The vow of obedience, by its very name, was the most obvious way of maintaining order on every level within our lives. When I made my profession, I promised God to obey the vows, and then I dutifully named all the legal entities who would chaperone me: the Rule of St. Augustine, the Constitutions of this Institute of St. Ursula, Canon Law, the Bull of our Holy Father, Paul V, and Reverend Mother. That was a lot of baggage for a young woman to carry.

The vow of Obedience taught us to be strong and independent through discipline. We were trained well to be thoughtful, to work hard, and to not expect undue praise or reward. We were to show our moral integrity through sacrifice and devotion and, especially, obedience to the higher values and virtues in life. Adversely, the vow also developed in us a certain childishness about responsibility and a dependence on our superiors. Since we were obedient daughters, we did not have adult responsibilities for many aspects of our lives, making significant decisions about where to live, what job to take, whom to love, even when and where we would eat or sleep or what kind of curtains we would hang in our bedroom. We were taxed sometimes with senseless rules and requirements, and often we were subject to arbitrary decisions over which we had no control.

Most seriously, and ultimately most harmfully, the vow of Obedience put us in a direct line of control that kept us subservient to a patriarchal institution. Jo Ann Kay McNamara says, "The Catholic clergy remains the last womenless space" (630). It is clear to many of us that the men fear women and fear that allowing them into their sacred space would destroy their power, perhaps even their masculine Church.

Out-of-order women, nuns, former nuns, married women, and single women think this last fear might be good for the Church. Women of all types might find a better deal in another church or community, one that thinks women deserve to be treated as fully grown, adult human beings. The male-dominated order might then be disturbed enough to reconsider its position about women. We believe that those of us who were and are out of order were harbingers of these ideas and changes within both church and society. Our task has been to work the metaphor, to help our sisters and our brothers within the Church and in our workplaces and neighborhoods and communities to understand the constraints of too much order. We are pushing the metaphor of being out of order as a way of saying that the former constructs of religious life and the role of women in the Catholic Church are outmoded, that being out of the old order is good, and that a newer order of life based on openness, love, and justice is the order of tomorrow.

Works Cited

Dante Alighieri. *The Divine Comedy.* Trans. Lawrence Grant White. New York: Pantheon Books, 1948.

Cavafy, Constantine. "Che Fece . . . Il Gran Rifiuto." *The Complete Poems of Cavafy.* Trans. Rae Dalven. NY: Harcourt Brace Jovanovich, 1976. 10.

McNamara, Jo Ann Kay. *Sisters in Arms: Catholic Nuns through Two Millennia.* Cambridge, Mass.: Harvard UP, 1996.

Oliver, Mary. "The Journey." *Dream Work.* NY: The Atlantic Monthly Press, 1986, 38–39.

Welty, Eudora. "The Worn Path." In *The Story and Its Writer.* 8th edition. Ed. Ann Charters. New York: Bedford/St. Martin's, 2011, 1360–1365.

Journey to Unruliness

Pat Montley

Once upon a time my heart was happy at St. Bernardine's Catholic Church in West Baltimore. For eight years, 1948 to 1956, I attended the parish school, where each day began with holy mass followed by religion class, a thorough and exquisitely Thomistic indoctrination in the Baltimore Catechism, which to this day occupies so much of my mental "k" that I no longer have room even for a new pin number. This simple, succinct book of religious instruction is a work of pure genius, its childlike Q&A format reinforcing the absolutism of its content. All questions neatly answered. No cause for fear or anxiety.

"Who are you?" it begins.

"I am a child of God."

"Why did God make you?"

"God made me to know Him, to love Him, and to serve Him in this life and to be happy with Him in the next."

What comfort!

By the fourth grade I was singing in the choir—conducted by the talented and charismatic Sister St. Jane—where I developed an undying passion for Gregorian chant. The only thing more fun than singing in the choir was performing in the school plays, directed by the adorably autocratic Sister Gabriel. By the seventh grade, I was chosen by the Grace-Kelly-serene Sister Robertine to be a sacristan, which meant I was privileged to spend my Saturday mornings scrubbing holy water fonts, scraping wax off candelabra, refilling little red votive lights, and, if very diligent in these mundane tasks, being allowed to lay out in the prescribed and ritual fashion the sacred vestments that the priests would wear the next morning.

I grew heady with the honor of it all and indeed felt very close to God. I knew every polished nook and cranny of that lovely church from the choir loft to the sacristy, and I felt a true ownership of it. I was happy to worship at its altar and put part of my allowance in the Sunday collection.

Thanks to a scholarship, I was whisked away from my working-class neighborhood (via a ninety-minute trip on three city buses twice a day) to the Other Side of the Tracks, where I attended Notre Dame Prep School, staffed by the School Sisters of Notre Dame. Here my talents (later to be in service to unruliness) were encouraged as I conscientiously applied them in my roles as class president, honors scholar, debater, actor, and athlete. Here, my Catholic roots went even deeper, my commitment to the work of the Church grew even stronger.

After graduating in 1960, I entered the convent, receiving my training at the SSND motherhouse and my BA in English at Notre Dame College, where I especially enjoyed the creative writing and drama classes. In the convent, my passion for ritual flourished. I loved chanting the divine office, singing high masses, writing and directing feast-day presentations that featured choral speaking.

I took first (temporary) vows in 1962. The Second Vatican Council was throwing open windows of opportunity, blowing out Catholicism's medieval cobwebs. John XXIII, dear man of great ecumenical vision and even greater heart, was pope; all was right with my world. But two books that came out of this wonderfully open and tragically short period in Catholic history would have a profound effect on my thinking.

One was *The Emerging Layman: The Role of the Catholic Layman in America* by Donald J. Thorman. (Never mind the sexist title; *Ms. Magazine* was still a decade away.) Thorman, perhaps inspired by the Vatican Council's official recognition of the "services and charismatic gifts of the laity," made it clear that one no longer had to be a priest or a nun to make a significant contribution to the work of the Church. I started asking myself: "What am I doing as a nun that I couldn't do as a lay person?"

The second book was *Authority in the Church* by the biblical scholar John L. McKenzie. So controversial was this book—viewed as heresy by some bishops—that I had to get special permission from my superior to read it. Yet what the book really challenged was not the church's authority, but its authoritarianism.

The section that resonated most with me was on the vow of obedience. I had had no trouble with poverty and chastity. (Who needs money and sex when you have God, right?!) But blind obedience? Doing what you are told for no better reason than that your superior said to? Where is the virtue in that?

Well, McKenzie, wily Jesuit that he was, pointed out that since those with a vow of obedience are required to obey their superiors in all things save sin, they must follow their own conscience if it conflicts with the order of a superior, and in order to do that, they are required to pass judgment on that order. Since passing such a judgment is antithetical to blind obedience, then the latter surely cannot be expected. My excitement at his lovely logic was surpassed only by my superiors' dismay. It was the beginning of the end of my conventual career. My questioning—of the nineteenth-century Rule and the archaic Customary Observances, with their authoritarian structures, suspicion of "The World," and resistance to change—persisted. In 1967, rather than take final vows, I left.

A year later, ready to embrace my calling as a "charismatic lay person," I headed for the University of Notre Dame, where McKenzie was on the theology faculty. Here I learned in church history classes about the nitty-gritty political realities and alliances that had sometimes shaped church doctrine and practice. I learned in scripture courses about canon selection and contextual interpretation and parallel myths. In Patristics class, I was appalled at the blatant misogyny of the Church fathers. I was amazed to discover in a class called Theological Anthropology that the experience that the mystics of my tradition described as "union with God" was the same experience Buddhists called *nirvana,* the same experience induced by Native Americans ingesting peyote mushrooms, and possibly the same experience enjoyed by Timothy O'Leary on LSD.

Nothing in the Baltimore Catechism had prepared me for this.

At the end of the year, armed with an MA in theology and disillusionment with my Catholic faith, I got a position teaching theology at Wheeling Jesuit College in West Virginia, where I lasted a year.

Happily (perhaps there *is* a god) I was rescued from the ravages of existential angst by my love for theater. While at Wheeling, I performed in plays sponsored by the English Department. My joy in this experience brought my heart home, reminding me of the exhilarating theatrical ventures of my grade school, high school, and even convent years. I determined to go back to graduate school, this time in theater. And so I did—a master's at Catholic University, a doctorate at Minnesota. This was followed by a career of writing and teaching and directing on college campuses until 2001, when I left teaching to devote my full energies to writing.

And what of my spiritual life? What happened on that front after I left South Bend, some 40+ years ago, disillusioned with the faith of my youth?

After the Notre Dame experience, I stayed away from church. During the 1970s, '80s, and '90s, it wasn't any church that provided my religion. Joachim Wach, author of *The Comparative Study of Religions,* holds that all religions, despite their wide variations, are characterized by three universal expressions: the theoretical—a system of belief; the practical—a system of worship; and the sociological—a system of social relationships.

It seems to me that belief systems are generally derived from stories of supernatural heroes. We believe in the importance of following the Ten Commandments because they were given to Moses by God on Mt. Sinai. Or we believe that Jesus was the son of God, was born of a virgin, and rose from the dead because that's what the divinely inspired story says. Or we accept the Buddha's way of salvation from suffering because the story tells us that while sitting under a bo tree he experienced the Great Enlightenment.

Or we believe the teachings of the Qur'an because it is the word of Allah, dictated by the Angel Gabriel to the Prophet Muhammad during an ecstatic experience. In each case, what gives the belief system its, well, credibility is its context of myth.

So I would re-phrase the three characteristics of religion identified by Joachim Wach—beliefs, worship, and social relationships. I would call them myth, ritual, and community. And those are indeed what I was looking for in a religion.

During much of those three decades, I found these three things working in theater, which, after all, is a creative community presenting in a ritualized way a story that has something meaningful to say. During those same decades I also found meaning, mission, and community in the feminist movement. So, as might be expected, I was having my most "religious experience" when writing and directing feminist plays.

And yet . . . and yet . . . I still longed for a religion like the Catholicism of my youth—something that was both absolutely reassuring and mysteriously sacred. But there was no going back. My brush with world religions had made it impossible for me ever again to espouse the limited dogmas or accept the limited gods of any one of them exclusively. Besides, thanks to a reactionary papacy, Catholicism had now to be ruled out not just on intellectual grounds but also on sociological ones. It seemed to me there was no comfortable place under its tent for feminists or homosexuals.

Around the mid-1990s I became aware of research done on goddess religions. What a delight to discover (with the help of Joseph Campbell and others) that, for millennia before a male god was imagined, people all over the world had worshipped a Great Goddess in one form or another. What exhilaration this brought me, following on my sense of betrayal by a patriarchal religion that had claimed my heart and then systematically trained me to devalue all that was female.

I started teaching a course on the Goddess in Myth and Ritual, lectured on the topic at a Women's Studies conference, and wrote plays about goddesses. This was an interest that my partner Sally shared, and so we went together on pilgrimages to goddess sites in Greece, Japan, Ireland, and England. We collected replicas of ancient artifacts reflecting reverence for goddesses. We created simple rituals for Sunday mornings that acknowledged the feminine divine, celebrated the changing of the seasons that reflected her role in nature, and developed an Earth-centered spirituality.

This went on for several years, and it helped to fill a void. But ultimately, to paraphrase T.S. Eliot, "it was (you might say) [not] satisfactory." For one thing, two people do not a community make. (Jewish custom required a *minyan* of ten men for certain types of prayer, and though Jesus is reputed to have said, "Where two or more of you are gathered in my name, there am I in the midst of them," he himself gathered at least twelve.)

Another reason our little dyadic services were not satisfactory was that we didn't really *worship* God the Mother, for in doing so we would have felt ourselves guilty of the same kind of idolatry that we had come to associate with worshipping God the Father—only, of course, it was wickedly more fun.

Ultimately, I came to believe that one should worship either all the deities or none. While worshipping all was more attractive aesthetically, and indeed could provide a sense of community with ancient and contemporary peoples all over the world, I felt that, for *me*, that option had become intellectually dishonest. If there is a consciousness greater than ours, an Oversoul, a Life Force, a Transcendent Spirit, surely it has to be more than a *personal* deity, an *Uber*-Parent, a super-sized version of the human.

So by the late '90s we were both restless. Sally wanted a church community with more than two people—people whom we could be there for and who would be there for us. And I wanted stimulating and meaningful services that didn't insist on a divine object of "worship."

So we explored. We explored the Quakers. Well, mostly *I* explored the Quakers. Sally the musician will have nothing to do with any religious group that doesn't *sing*. But the Friends' social action orientation appealed to my sense of social responsibility. And their emphasis on silent meditation appealed to the contemplative side of me that had been happily nurtured in my convent years. I must say I always enjoyed Quaker meeting. But when it was over, I was ready for "church." It seemed like meditation before mass, the warm-up before the big event; only for them, the meditation *was* the big event. Sadly, I concluded that for my ritual-hungry spirit, this would not do.

Then we explored the Unitarians—several different congregations—and finally settled in the First Unitarian Church of Baltimore, a two-hundred-year-old urban church thirty minutes from our suburban home. Have I found in this denomination the "absolutely reassuring and mysteriously sacred" religion that I longed for? Alas, no. Have I found the richness of "myth, ritual, and community" that I hoped would feed my spirit? Well, I'm learning to live with one out of three. Unitarians have little in the way of myth and ritual, but it didn't hurt that the publishing arm of the Unitarian Universalist Association enthusiastically accepted my proposal to write a book on just that subject and that the minister of the Baltimore church invited me to write and conduct a Winter Solstice Ritual there, which has since become an annual event.

What I *have* found in Unitarian Universalism is a fitting spiritual home, that is, one that fits many of my spiritual needs. Why?

First, because of its seven principles, which affirm: the inherent worth and dignity of every person; justice, equity, and compassion in human relations; acceptance of one another and encouragement to spiritual growth; a free and responsible search for truth and meaning; the right of conscience and the use of the democratic process within our congregations and in society at large; the goal of world community with peace, liberty, and justice for all; and respect for the interdependent web of all existence. This is the only "creed" I can bring myself to profess.

Many of these principles—though perhaps described in different language—are consistent with the Gospel I learned in my early Catholicism. The others stretch me in the direction I desire to go.

Second, in my Unitarian-Universalist church, Sunday services are celebrations of life, "worship" services only in the etymological sense of the word: celebrating what has "worth" or value—the natural world, our human relationships, our search for and creation of meaning.

Third, my "downtown" Baltimore congregation is racially, culturally, and religiously diverse, and committed to social action. Many of us are "hyphenated" UU's, identifying also as humanists, Christians, Buddhists, atheists, or Wiccans. We march for civil rights, campaign for a living wage for hourly workers, agitate for affordable housing, cook for the local soup kitchen, and provide hands-on support for a local housing program and for neighborhood direct services. We write letters to the editor, collect signatures, and bang on the doors of our state legislators. And we see this as part of our "spiritual practice."

We respect and care for, argue with and challenge one another. And we see this as part of our spiritual practice.

We are unruly. And it feels . . . *right*.

Ironically, I owe my journey to unruliness to the Catholic Church. From Sister Annella's insistence to us third-graders that "The most important question is 'Why?,'" to Sister Paul Mary's insistence that we high school debaters have the facts at our fingertips to argue either side of a topic, to Sister Maura's insistence that our college English term papers reflect original critical thinking, the training in my Catholic school classrooms—despite the authoritarianism of the Church and the Religious Life—promoted a vigorous curiosity, an intellectual rigor, a fierce honesty, an untiring discipline. These very things—applied to the Church's teachings and structures—proved the undoing of my faith. But they have served me well in my unruly life.

So here I am at 70+—a Unitarian ex-nun lesbian grandmother playwright . . . which means I have spent much of my life confronting and trying to resolve conflict—in the context of a dramatically changing world. This is reflected in my lifelong obsession with values: how they are formed, challenged, changed; what happens when they are inadequate, misguided, conflicting. Thus, the themes of my plays include faith and forgiveness, religion and repression, challenging authority and cherishing mentors, seeking justice and celebrating spirit. Because the strongest—and equal—influences on my life and art have been my Catholic upbringing and the feminist movement, the conflict between these two is explored in a number of my works. Perhaps ironically, this conflict has also developed my sense of humor, which informs not just my playful satires but even my serious dramas.

I have made painful choices in my life: abandoning beliefs that once provided solace and solidarity; choosing a different path from those I once trod with family, dear friends, and valued teachers; breaking from a tradition that was critical to the formation of my identity. None of this has been easy. The unruly life is not a comfortable one. But for me it is the only honest one.

The Renunciation

Pat Montley

Lights come up on ELIZABETH, humming and dusting in the nursery. She is pregnant, leaning over a cradle.

MARY: (*Offstage.*) Hello! Is anybody home?

ELIZ: I'm in here—in the nursery.

MARY: (*Entering, with a basket containing packages.*) Cousin Lizzie! (*They embrace in front of the dresser.*)

ELIZ: Well, Mary darling! How good to see you! Are you off for spring break to be free for trekking all the way down here in the middle of March?

MARY: No, Cousin Lizzie. I graduated high school last June. Don't you remember? You and Cousin Zachary sent me a lovely pottery wheel. Didn't you get my thank-you note?

ELIZ: Well, of course I did, Mary. That's just how forgetful I am lately. It's true what they say—old age brings on the senility.

MARY: In your case it seems to have brought on something else too.

ELIZ: Yes, wasn't that a surprise?

MARY: I'll bet. (*Crosses to cradle.*) Just think—the first menopause baby in our family. What did Cousin Zachary say when you told him?

ELIZ: As you can imagine, it left him . . . speechless.

MARY: No doubt.

ELIZ: And let me tell you, Mary, he has reason to be.

MARY: What do you mean?

ELIZ: This is no menopause baby. This is a prayer baby.

MARY: What?

ELIZ: Listen, honey, most folks don't know my age because I try to take care of myself—you know, keep myself nice and all—going in to Ain Karim every Saturday to get my hair done and that sort of thing. But fact is, I'm sixty years old.

MARY: Sixty!

ELIZ: What's more, it's been a long time since Zachary saw sixty. And a longer time since he saw any action.

MARY: You mean—

ELIZ: I mean this little bugger came directly from the Big G. herself.

MARY: But that's most unusual.

ELIZ: You can say that again. Most folks wouldn't believe it. That's why we're not making an issue of it. I'm sure you understand.

MARY: You mean you just asked God for a baby, and . . . *bang!*?

ELIZ: It's a lot easier than the other way, I can tell you that. Especially when you're sixty.

MARY: But didn't God have any misgivings about—

ELIZ: None at all. In fact, she thought it was a marvelous idea. Wondered why she hadn't thought of doing it that way in the first place. Mumbled something about her experiment being a failure.

MARY: Her experiment?

ELIZ: (*Crosses to a bucket on top of a stool.*) Yes. Project Andros or Mandros or some such name. She didn't go into it much. (*Starts swishing brush around in pail.*) Anyway, she promised me the baby, and sure enough . . .

MARY: (*Crossing to ELIZ.*) And sure enough, you shouldn't be doing all this housework, Lizzie. Now give me that apron.

ELIZ: (*Crosses behind MARY, squeezing her shoulders as she crosses.*) You're a real doll, Mary. Always have been. (*Taking off apron and giving it to MARY.*) Many's the time I said so to your Mama. And to think how she wanted a boy. Just goes to show you.

MARY: Listen, Cousin Lizzie, I brought you some things in the basket there. Stopped off at the deli on the way over for some lox and bagels. Why don't you put them away? I'll finish this. (*Puts on apron.*)

ELIZ: (*Crossing to basket.*) Why thank you, Mary. That was sweet of you. (*Takes up basket and starts out.*) Speaking of food—you know, I've had some of the strangest cravings lately. You won't believe this: yesterday I was positively pining for—of all things—locusts and wild honey!

(*They laugh as ELIZ exits. MARY starts humming and dusting the dresser. An enormous, gum-chewing woman enters. It is GABRI-ELLA. She looks around and then nods confidently.*)

GAB: Hello there, Mary.

MARY: Oh, hello.

GAB: The door was open.

MARY: Are you from the neighborhood?

GAB: Well, in a way. This is my precinct.

MARY: Are you a Security Guard?

GAB: Yes, as a matter of fact, I am. But today I'm working more in the capacity of a Messenger.

MARY: Please come in, won't you. (*Starting to leave.*) My cousin is in the next room—I'll get her. I'm just visiting here.

GAB: But it's you I came to see.

MARY: Me?

GAB: Yes, I've heard some wonderful things about you.

MARY: Oh?

GAB: My name is Gabriella. (*They shake hands.*)

MARY: Glad to meet you.

GAB: (*Displaying her wing-sleeves.*) I'm an angel.

MARY: An angel! You don't say! I've never met an angel before.

GAB: Well, we hope you'll be seeing a lot of me in future.

MARY: We?

GAB: God and I. It's God who told me the wonderful things about you. It was her idea to send me to you with the message.

MARY: The message?

GAB: Well, actually, it's more of an invitation.

MARY: Invitation?

GAB: Why do you keep repeating everything I say?

MARY: Oh, I am sorry—it's just that I'm a bit taken by surprise. Please forgive me for being rude. (*Gestures toward a chair.*) Won't you sit down? Would you like something to drink? Or some fresh lox and bagels?

GAB: No—no, thank you. I never eat.

MARY: Gracious! You got to look like that without eating?

GAB: (*"Displaying" herself.*) Well, actually, I don't look like this. I don't look like anything. This is the shape I chose to assume for the occasion.

MARY: Of all possible shapes, you chose that one?

GAB: Yes. You see, one of my pet movements is Fat People's Liberation. I try to do my part to break down the prejudice against obesity whenever I get the chance.

MARY: I see.

GAB: But it's another movement I came to talk to you about today.

MARY: Yes, what is this "invitation" you mentioned before?

GAB: All right. (*Jumps up on dresser and assumes an "annunciation" pose.*) Here it is: God has authorized me to offer you . . . the saviorship of the world!

MARY: The what?

GAB: The saviorship of the world! (*Hops down.*) She wants you to be the messiah.

MARY: But I'm only seventeen.

GAB: Youth is an asset.

MARY: And I have no experience.

GAB: Innocence is an asset.

MARY: I haven't even been to college yet.

GAB: Education is *not* an asset.

MARY: But I'm a woman.

GAB: Ah, that is the greatest asset of all.

MARY: Do you think my fiancé would agree to it?

GAB: If he wouldn't, he shouldn't be your fiancé. And anyway—we're talking about *you*. This is *your* decision.

MARY: I know, I know. (*Crosses to bucket.*) But I guess I've just been so socialized, I'd have to consult my man. (*Begins to scrub floor.*)

GAB: Well, listen Mary, it's time you had your consciousness raised. Men have been screwing up the world for millennia now. Everyplace you look, things are a mess. Why, just consider your own situation. The people are overtaxed while the Romans make millions publishing Caesar's boring battlefield diaries. And while the world rots, the theologians bicker in the synagogue. (*Sits.*) Now I ask you.

MARY: (*Straightens up on her knees.*) I really would like to do my part. In fact, I've already applied to Rabbi Seminary. Just had my SAT scores sent in last week. I should be hearing from them soon.

GAB: Oh, you'll hear from them, all right. What you'll hear from them is a loud "No" and the suggestion that you see a shrink.

MARY: Still . . . I'd prefer to work within the system for change. (*Resumes scrubbing.*)

GAB: The system is corrupt beyond redemption, Mary. Why, just a few months ago God admitted—I heard her say this myself—that Project Andros has failed. I tell you, Mary, we're up for revolution now. It's time for Project Gynekos. That's where you fit in.

MARY: (*Straightening again.*) God wants me to head Project Gynekos? To lead the revolution?

GAB: Exactly. Although the socio-religio-political system is beyond redemption, God would like to save the world. And, truth is, she's had it with flood and fire purgations. Not only are they somewhat extremist and a great deal of trouble, but they don't work.

MARY: What *will* work?

GAB: You tell me.

MARY: (*Getting up.*) Hmm . . . maybe if the tyrants could be brought to a change of heart through reason and love . . .

GAB: Hooray! Now—who are the most reasonable and loving creatures in the world?

MARY: Why, women, of course.

GAB: Right again. And the most reasonable and loving woman is . . . YOU! So how about it, Mar?

MARY: But who would accept a woman messiah?

GAB: Well, for a start—other women.

MARY: Are you kidding? They've all been so socialized, they'd be the first to object. No, no, there's a lot of groundwork to be done before we're ready for that move.

GAB: (*Sits.*) Well, what do you suggest?

MARY: I know! Let me have a son. He can be the messiah.

GAB: A son! What a cop-out. You're feeding right into the corrupt system.

MARY: No, no! *My* son will be different. I'll train him to be liberated.

GAB: Ha! That's what they all said. Eve and Sarah and Rebecca and Rachel and Bathsheba—the whole crowd of them had big ideas for training their sons. But it just doesn't work. I tell you, something's wrong with their basic makeup. A design flaw. Even God admits it.

MARY: But my son *will* be different.

GAB: Why?

MARY: Well because . . . for one thing, I'll get him the new way. (*Points to cradle.*)

GAB: What new way?

MARY: You know—Elizabeth's way.

75

GAB: Oh, that. Well, I suppose it would make a little difference. But he'd still be a man.

MARY: Oh, come on—trust me. (*Offers to shake hands.*) Is it a deal?

GAB: It's a compromise, that's what it is. You're sure you won't take the job yourself? (*MARY shakes her head. GAB reluctantly crosses to her.*) Well, all right then.

MARY & GAB: (*Together, shaking hands.*) So be it.

GAB: But I still think it's a cop-out. You'll see, Mary. Your boy will make mistakes like the rest of them. For one thing, if the revolution succeeds and he gets into office, he'll appoint a cabinet of all men. And then there'll be dissention among them and jockeying for power until the whole administration goes corrupt from within.

MARY: Oh, come on now—don't be so pessimistic.

GAB: I'm telling you, that's what will happen. And the repercussions will last so long, it'll be another two thousand years before Project Gynekos can be tried.

MARY: Well, maybe you're right after all. Who knows? Anyway, in another two thousand years the world will surely be ready for it.

GAB: (*Crosses to MARY, puts a hand on her shoulder. They both face out.*) I hope so, Mary . . . I hope so.

(*Lights down.*)

Note

"The Renunciation" is a scene from *Bible Herstory*, available from Samuel French, Inc. http://www.samuelfrench.com/

Polishing the Brass

Liz Dolan

After evening prayers, when all the other Sisters recreated in the main house, I crept up the steep oak stairs to S. Gerard's cell. I knocked on her door and handed her a leather suitcase filled with outdated clothes: a blue shirtwaist dress, a nylon slip, a trench coat, and penny loafers. After she changed into the secular clothes, she tapped on the door, signaling me to enter, an action forbidden until now. When I saw her, I guffawed. It was 1968, but she looked like something from the '50s. The dress brushed her ankles, the cuffs hid her wrists, the shoes were clunky, and a cowlick crowned her chopped brunette hair.

"I can tell by your face what I must look like," Gerard said.

"Good thing we have no mirrors, Alfalfa," I grinned, trying to quell the sadness I was feeling. "At least you won't have to worry about any of the late-night Romeos hitting on you in Grand Central."

"Gee, thanks for the support, S. Ann."

"You may not have to leave, Gerard," I blurted out, even though I knew it was stupid to raise her hopes.

"Why not?"

"Because I asked S. Catherine to intercede for you. She's probably talking to Mother right now."

On her cot, Gerard had carefully folded her long white gown, scapular, wimple, belt, and rosary. On the back of the oak chair hung the stiff, dome-like black veil lined in white that had made her look more beautiful than she really was. Without it Gerard looked diminished, bird-like. I detached the silver crucifix from the rosary and handed it to her.

"Funny, I don't even know why you're being sent home, Gerard."

"Because Mother Daniel said I don't have a communal personality, whatever that means. Did you tell her I was neglecting the chapel?"

"Never. Why are you even asking me that question?" I felt hurt that my childhood friend could think that of me.

"Well, Mother knew all about the unwashed linens and the tarnished candles. I figured you told her, Ann, because sometimes I think the rules are more important to you than people. Beware, pal, you may turn into a S. Dominic." Gerard sat on the edge of her cot smoothing her hair.

"What's wrong with Dominic? She's a model nun, a scholar."

"Yes, she is, but God forbid a postulant puts the fork on the wrong side of her plate. All hell breaks loose."

"You exaggerate, Gerard."

"I sit opposite her in the refectory. She moves silently, has custody of the eyes, never allows her glance to stray, but I always feel she scorns most of her Sisters. She's not a model. She's proud, all about rules."

"But we have to follow The Rule."

"Not if it makes you lose yourself."

"We're supposed to lose ourselves, Gerard."

"I lost myself, Ann, and became as cold and tough as steak. But I prayed and prayed and one day I realized God wanted me to be me, giving whatever natural talent I have to help others." She fingered the rosary on top of her clothing pile as if she knew her prayers had not been wasted.

"But you had been doing that all along, Gerard. Look how you care for the kids in the orphanage."

"Yes, but I was always conflicted, thinking I was breaking The Rule because I was too attached to them. Then I started really breaking The Rule like a rebellious adolescent, neglecting my duties and skipping devotions."

"Why didn't you tell me you were struggling with all this?"

"Because I thought you were too busy being perfect. Ann, have you ever thought about why you entered?"

"Every single day." I folded my arms under my scapular.

"Maybe 'cause your father was a tyrant?"

"Your father was no bargain either, Dr. Freud."

"You're right, he was a broken-down old drunk who wasn't around very much. But when he was sober he was sweet and loving. That's why I took his name."

"Gerard, I love and pity my father. My mother told me he lost his mother young, and in the old country there were days when he ate nothing but seaweed. One day, I realized he needed me more than I needed him. Maybe I became a nun so I could pray for him."

"Maybe you became a nun 'cause he demanded too much from you or to get away from him. Just think about it, is all I'm saying, Ann. I worry. Is this the right place for you?"

"Maybe you should worry about yourself, Gerard, about adjusting to the outside world after being in a convent for four long years. Sorry, sorry for my big mouth, I take that back. I know Mother will listen to S. Catherine."

"Mother isn't going to change her mind. S. Catherine was indulging you. Don't worry about me. I'm still me. When Mother told me I was being sent home because I had trouble with obedience, I asked her what obedience was. One day we were told off for not obeying no matter how absurd the command, and the next day we were in trouble because we obeyed blindly. What were we supposed to do?"

"What did she say?"

"Absolutely nothing, I guess my questions proved to her that I did have trouble with obedience. But after I spoke with her I had a dream I was auditioning for The Rockettes. A cigar-smoking, fire-plug of a man tossed me a hot pink costume dripping with spangles. I slipped into the shimmering line of legs and arms, chugging like a locomotive, tapping down a narrow wrought-iron spiral staircase, metal polishing metal." Gerard tapped her feet softly, telling her dream in rhythm to her tapping. "We slid onto a revolving stage. It was the wrong stage! We kept tapping. And a 5 and a 6 and a 7 and an 8, and a 5 and a 6 and a 7 and an 8. Heads held high, we tapped backward up and up and up the corkscrew stairs, darker and narrower at each turn, gears greased and humming, our breathing shallow." Gerard caught her breath.

"Suddenly I turned around; I had to mount the stairs alone, covering little ground, but still climbing upward, toward the light."

"You should see your face, you look like you had a vision. Why, you're happy you're leaving," I said, my mouth agape.

"I did have a vision; God was telling me I needed to go home—that's where I belong. Mother's right. There are plenty of kids outside who need me. But you have a gift for study, Ann. How will you become a scholar when you never express your own thoughts? The Ann I used to know is getting lost. You're from the old neighborhood; you used to have spunk. Remember when we played stickball together and we'd beat the pants off the boys every chance we got?"

I remembered Gerard whacking the ball over the fence in the concrete backyard and yelling at the opposing team, "Match that, suckers!" as her long skinny legs carried her body around the bases. And I would echo, jumping up and down, my fist raised, "Match that, suckers!" I had always been Gerard's cheerleader. But I never had her courage.

"I can't think about anything right now except that I'm going to miss you," I said, choking on my tears.

"Gotta go, Ann; the taxi's here." Gerard hugged me as she tightened the belt of the potato-sack trench coat around her waist. "I'm gonna miss you, too." She flew down the rickety stairs, out the oak door, and under the arches of the wrought-iron gate to the waiting taxi.

I ran down after her. Before she ducked her head to enter the cab, Gerard spun around and took a last look at the brick portals of the cloister. I recalled a feisty ten-year-old, out of breath, sweating, plaiting her loosened braids after a heated tryst of Double Dutch. I could hear her saying, "I have to get this hair cut, Ann; it slows me down."

At breakfast the next morning, Sister Gerard's place setting had been removed. I knew her name would not be mentioned again. That was as it should be; the good of the community came first. But I also knew convent life would never be the same without her. I pondered over what Gerard had said about my father— maybe I *had* entered to get away from him. But I would've left home sooner or later, anyway. Maybe I entered because I feared I would marry someone just like him. Maybe I entered because I wanted to have a scholarly life, and I knew children would interfere with that. I was confused.

Since I had only three months before profession of vows, I had to think things through. Did I enter to do God's work or my own? Had the life suited me so well because I was really self-indulgent? Did I repress my true self, as Gerard had said, because I wanted my superiors to think highly of me? And if I did, was that so terrible?

One thing I knew for sure: Gerard had always been a kinder and more truthful nun than I had ever been. Even as a kid, she was that way. I remembered the day hulking Danny Garrido, who was always pulling my braids in school, knocked me down in the middle of a stickball game. Gerard dropped the stick and shouted in his face: "The reason you act like such a jerk with her, Danny, is because you like her." I was terrified that Danny was going to deck Gerard; he wasn't use to being yelled at, especially by a girl. Instead Danny, beet-red, pulled his cap off his head, the size of a football, skulked out of the schoolyard, and never bothered me again. I never could have said that to him, even though I knew he liked me. Plus I was afraid of him. Gerard was never afraid of speaking the truth or defending anyone who needed it.

As I watched the postulant in her somber black dress place the basket of rolls at the end of the oblong table, I remembered when Gerard and I were postulants walking down the aisles of the refectory in front of Mother, the professed Sisters and novices. We balanced the basins of hot water, which we placed on the end of each table, where the Sisters passed their dishes to be washed with a small rag mop. When we returned to the pantry, we shook with nervous laughter, amazed we had survived the gauntlet.

Aligning my napkin with the folds in my scapular, I smoothed it on my lap and took a roll from the basket, signed the letter B for butter on the table so a Sister would pass it to me. Then I hooked the same finger, raised it, the sign for the pitcher of milk without distracting anyone from the reading. Although the thought of apologizing today to Mother for questioning her decision terrified me, I would also tell her that for the first time I was questioning my vocation and that I still thought it was a mistake to send Gerard home—that her absence diminished all of us.

This evening I'd also confess my fault before my Sisters, falling to my knees, prostrating myself in the chapel aisle, as I ate the floor's dust. But first I would polish the lusterless brass candles so that their glow would ignite charity and courage in my heart, the courage I'd surely need, now that Gerard was gone.

Timing

Patricia M. Dwyer

At 18.

September 12, 1969. Philadelphia, PA.

The crushed gravel crackled as we drove up the long driveway leading to Fontbonne Hall, where I would spend the next nine months studying to be a Sister of St. Joseph. The scratchy gabardine postulant gown I had donned a few hours earlier felt foreign and otherworldy. My parents in the front seat of the car were quiet and subdued. This was the moment of leave-taking, and while a level of excitement or anticipation had filled our home as I readied myself, this mood was different. What to expect?

The postulant director, Sister Frances Anita, greeted us at the door. She had a large, fill-the-room kind of presence. Her smile was warm and genuine. We were led into a large room with circles of folding chairs—one arced seating area for each postulant and teary family members saying their last goodbyes.

What was I doing here? Having turned an idealistic eighteen during the turbulent and exhilarating 1960s, I yearned to make a difference in the world. While not terribly religious, I grew up one of five children in a relatively traditional Catholic family. Our world in suburban Philadelphia was Catholic. *The Baltimore Catechism* did nothing to inspire me, but wafts of incense, Gregorian chant, and sounding chimes offered the ritual and symbol that resonated with me.

Inspired by several Sisters of Joseph who were energetic young women—vibrant and smart, creative and committed to their mission—I felt a "calling." It is hard now to discern how my own "subtexts" played into this decision. I was not particularly attracted to boys growing up, and the community of women felt comfortable and safe. In 1969, with fewer options for women and careers, perhaps this seemed like a good opportunity. The attention I gained when announcing my desire to enter the convent made me feel "special"—an ache growing out of middle-child syndrome? Who knows?

Sister Frances led us into a large room that screamed discomfort. The gray metal folding chairs were hard and cold. My brothers in suit and ties, sister in a Sunday dress, and parents more sober than proud. Conversation was formal as we groped for topics to keep our minds off the inevitable goodbyes. The gong sounded, and Mother Frances raised her hands to call us forth. My new life had begun.

With this new life came new routines: early rising, community dining, quiet and communal prayer, walks "in open," and limits on time for conversation with my new Sisters. I was fortunate to enter when I did. Post–Vatican II Council, many of the trappings of the old church were being relinquished for more relevant religious practices. Priests faced us at Mass rather than turning their backs. Mysterious Latin phrases translated into English prayers. Guitars and folk songs replaced organs and traditional hymns. The Vatican Council shifted the focus from hierarchy to humanity, and the impact was nothing short of transformational.

In Fontbonne Hall, we new postulants experienced these changes as welcome, while some of the older Sisters grimaced with displeasure at every twang of the guitar we played at Mass. With the Council's blessing, rote prayers were gradually abandoned in favor of more biblically based morning prayer and evening vespers. Studying mystics like St. Theresa of Avila and John of the Cross became the norm, and my prayer life, feeble as it was, was turned on its head as I learned more about meditation, spirituality, and an interior life I discovered in myself.

At 39.

January 3, 1991. Washington, D.C.
Somehow, turning thirty-nine years old became a threshold, a line I would not go past without dealing with my "issues." I had been a Sister of St. Joseph since 1969. Having entered the convent at eighteen years of age, I had very little, if any, idea of the person I was or who I would become.

Life-changing events punctuated my twenty-one years as a Sister of St. Joseph. My father's death in 1984. My decision to attend Middlebury College's Bread Loaf School of English rather than the typical choice for nuns at the time—Notre Dame University in South Bend, Indiana. Serving in multiple leadership roles and living a "successful" Sister's life.

Beneath the veneer of success, however, my inner life was turbulent. Another, more secretive theme in my religious life was a string of romantic relationships I had had with various Sisters with whom I had lived. My outside life witnessed vows of poverty, chastity, and obedience; my inward life was tortured by guilt at my duplicity. At the same time, I was experiencing a certain awakening about my sexuality that had never been realized before my developmentally naïve eighteen-year-old self became a Sister. I had several brushes with crushes, and I knew the excitement of surreptitious glances and clandestine meetings late in the evening in cubicles separated by curtains meant to discourage such encounters.

But even in these multiple romantic and sometimes sexual relationships, I never saw myself as gay. Early on, I convinced myself (and was told by mentors I approached about my "problem") that postulants and novices live in a "hot house" situation. This attraction was normal. Once I got through the first few years of living with women similar in age, I would join the real world of teaching and living in a conventional convent life. The feelings would go away. But they didn't. In some way, I carefully separated my secret life from the idea of being gay and the stigma attached. I could acknowledge my moral failures, but putting them in the same context as homosexuality was more shameful than I could bear.

In 1981, while deciding on a school for my master's in English, I resisted the idea of Notre Dame—I wanted a dramatic difference from the environment of nuns and priests that I typically inhabited. One of my college professors suggested Bread Loaf. I was intrigued by the name alone, and then discovered the school's Robert Frost roots and preeminent writing institute. Along with more than two hundred theater, writing, and literature students studying on Bread Loaf Mountain every summer for seven weeks, I found my eyes opened and my world stretched. I met gay men (and became lifelong friends with one in particular) and lesbians, poets, and players. I went to parties (one year, at a "Suppressed Desire" party, as Pat Benatar), wore makeup, and soaked in difference from my life as a nun.

Throughout my thirties I was on something of an emotional rollercoaster. I would have upheavals, usually triggered by one of my summers at school or a relationship in which I found myself, and plunge into waves of doubt and guilt. Then I would fortify my successful nun persona: completing a rewarding and fulfilling six years as a coordinator at a convent with ten other Sisters, getting elected to participate in congregational governance meetings, and starting a PhD program in American Literature at George Washington University.

Here I was, at thirty-nine, holding these two lives in anything but a balance. Turning forty loomed. I simply could not face another decade without facing myself. I decided to take a leave of absence from the community that had supported and nurtured me, a community that I loved and in which I met many of my dearest friends. Three months later, I came out to my family. My father's death seven years earlier made this dramatic move easier. While a devoted and loving father, he was a strong supporter of preserving image. For him, my coming out would have been a terrible blow to the family face of Catholic loyalty and conventional values. I will never know how he would have responded, and so I try to imagine the best. My traditional Catholic mother, however, said, "I love you no matter what." Brothers and sisters followed suit. Nieces and nephews embraced me. The circle of love stretched to include the gay daughter, sister, and aunt who was an ex-nun.

At 63.

October 15, 2014. Baltimore, MD.

After leaving the convent, I continued in my career dedicated to education. With a PhD in hand, I started teaching at the college level, while taking on administrative roles that demanded progressively more responsibility, from Dean to Associate Vice President to Provost at three different institutions.

At the same time, I was committed to being honest about my life. In 2005, I celebrated a civil union with the wonderful woman who is now my wife. There was no job that could make me compromise my commitment to her or our union together. I know that has limited some of my opportunities for career advancement over the years, and I am saddened that many gay people feel it necessary to hide their relationships so they can break through the proverbial pink ceiling. But I would never change my decision. In fact, when being offered my current position six years ago, I was on the phone with the president of the college, and I confided that I was gay and in a committed relationship. I did not want to blindside him. No surprises. I almost cried at his response: "I want the best person for the job, and I believe that person is you. Nothing else really matters."

Yesterday, I heard on the radio that seven additional states will be granting marriage licenses to same-sex couples. That means thirty-two states in all. Pope Francis is holding a summit at the Vatican on the family as I write, and the Bishops' reflections about gays and divorced Catholics have taken a more conciliatory and inclusive tone. No longer are homosexuals the "intrinsically evil" segment of society the church had previously condemned. Societal divisions, criticism, and exclusion are disintegrating on so many levels, and our young people lead the way in denouncing prejudice and advocating for equality.

But, for me, I could no longer be a Catholic. I could not be part of a religion that revered my role in its hierarchy at one moment and so quickly excluded me when I uttered one simple fact: "I'm gay." For this reason, it was easy to distinguish my feelings about leaving the church versus leaving the convent. Leaving the church liberated me. Saying no to an institution that so marginalized me gave me strength. In my religious life, however, I saw committed women who believed in their mission to serve the poor, who valued educational excellence, who translated church liturgy in creative and sometimes revolutionary ways. As a nun, I saw the Sisters' role as separate from the church, one that challenged and questioned from within. And now in 2014, they continue on that path, but in a more forceful and public way. The nuns of today have met the church's criticism and suspicions head on. While working toward reconciliation with the hierarchy, they do not waver in their values of inclusion, women's rights, and dedication to society's outcasts. The hypocrisy of the church in this regard astounds me, that this scandal-ridden institution targets those who are closest to Jesus' message of love and forgiveness.

My life is whole and rich. I have a devoted and loving spouse, and we are solid in our commitment to each other. From my years with the Sisters, I came to understand the importance of an interior life, and I have often relied on Buddhist traditions and meditation to ground me in nurturing that spirit. I remain committed to improving our educational systems, and work at a college that welcomes and supports a high percentage of minority students and those who are first in their families to go to college. My leadership skills are built on the experiences I had with the Sisters, emphasizing collaboration and communal participation. All of this has served me well, and I am grateful for the part the congregation played in shaping my life. I continue to admire the nuns and their commitment to the values that attracted me to them in the first place. We remain sisters.

I Am a Catholic Nun

Sharon Kanis

I am a Catholic nun. It has been fifty years since I professed my vows of poverty, celibacy, and obedience. What I thought that meant in 1964 and what I think now differ wildly! Recently I was invited to submit a reflection of my experience as an "unruly" Catholic nun. Now I ask myself: Am I unruly?

Would you have considered me unruly in 1968, when I was available to my twelfth-grade student as she felt the need to unburden her conscience? She and two classmates had been selling marijuana to first-year students. She directed me to retrieve their stash from the chapel tabernacle. My community of seven marveled that we had an opportunity to study the "stash" until the police came to claim it. To my student's credit, she stood tall even as she withstood the anger of her co-conspirators and accepted the consequences of her actions.

My community, School Sisters of Notre Dame, espouse the vision that "the education of women is the transformation of the world." In my hands, does education become unruly? During my early teaching career, when I realized that most of my students who attended our Catholic school, with a student body who were 99 percent white, had never had a conversation with a person of color, I decided to initiate a nontraditional educational experience.

Every Saturday morning, a dozen white high school girls and I traveled to the segregated black section of town to play in the public playground. There we joined the neighborhood children, sharing sweets and stories until we became fast friends. I can still picture the row of young children sitting on the curb waiting for our unlikely entourage to arrive to play.

Some of my sisters in community thought me unruly when I responded to an invitation from another student (in another city) to join a public demonstration protesting injustice. It was 1972; my student was a lifeguard at a private pool whose members were primarily Catholic. She had become aware that the pool had a policy restricting membership to whites only. In fact, African Americans were not even permitted as guests. My white student's righteous indignation sparked my own, and I was honored to join her in my full habit on the picket line, to the consternation of some of my students' parents and at least one of my community members. Did I, as an educator and nun, raise my student's awareness, or did she raise mine? Clearly the latter. I'm happy to add that this student continues to be a public advocate for justice in my city.

My sisters in community were not the only ones keeping an eye on me. Once when I joined a protest against the policies of an elected official in Baltimore, I noticed that my dad was driving by, motioning to me to get into the car. Thinking an emergency had happened at home, I complied. My dad said, "Your mother saw you on the news and said, 'Go and get her!'" Needless to say, I was not happy.

One summer in the early 1970s, a Sister friend and I agreed to honor the invitation (again by students) to make ourselves available to those who would be working a summer job at a local beach resort. For most, this was their first extended time away from home, and they were both excited and scared. My friend and I also had a job in a Christmas shop where we were given a vivid taste of the culture of the young. (We were no longer wearing habits.) Our students and their friends knew we were there for them; they visited often, and also came in times of crisis or homesickness to be in a safe space with adults they trusted. Mutual gifting all around!

Perhaps there is an unruly nature to my spiritual life as well. I was raised solidly in the tradition, and my spiritual practice was formed by the culture of my religious community. I longed to be faithful to my prayer life as it had been modeled for me. But God moves in unexpected ways. One day when I was walking alone, I had a profound experience that was for me like wandering into a parable: I saw an old woman sitting at a loom, weaving with silver threads. She was beautiful and vibrant and wore a simple brown robe. She said, "Don't worry. I am here and my work is being done. Let the powers do as they must." By this, I understood her to mean global, political, church, and community leaders who sometimes act in contradiction to God's desires. She continued, "I am very busy and my work is being done. I am connecting you to one another." Then I saw the people of the world connected through their hearts by a fine silver thread. I realized that the thread she was weaving to connect us was her own silver hair. Now I know only one thing for certain: God is not as we think.[1]

Some of these situations stand out in my memory because they are not typical. But I suspect my true unruly nature has been best expressed in classrooms populated by college students during the past twenty-five years. I have my sights set on what could be, not on what is. If I am teaching my students about poverty, let's hear directly from a single mom who raised her family in the projects and found her voice and her power there. If I am offering a course about marriage in its religious and spiritual contexts, let's invite divorced, remarried, and lesbian couples as well as the long married. If our topic is Sacraments, why not design our own sacrament that would meet our spiritual needs as well as those of others in our circle? If these practices qualify as unruly, then I hope that all education is unruly.

I identify myself in many ways. I am woman. I am daughter, sister, friend. I am teacher and student. I am singer, dancer, reader, skier, gardener. I love to eat and to feed others, friends and strangers alike. I weep at true accounts of heartache and sad movies. I rage at injustice as I perceive it. I rejoice in every season and in every kind of weather. As with each of us, I am more than the sum of my parts. I am Catholic. I am Sister. I am nun.

I guess you could say I am unruly.

Note

1. This experience also appears in *Cloud of Witnesses*. Edited by Joan S. Hickey. Minneapolis: Seraphina Press, 2012. 172.

Faith in the Wasteland

Christine Schenk

My Mother/Father Myself

Actually, I've always been a justice person. It came with the territory if you grew up in the Joan and Paul Schenk family. We weren't poor exactly, but with four daughters close in age, and my Dad a returning World War II Purple Heart hero who hated the very thought of college, money was at a premium.

We lived in Lima, Ohio, where Dad sold life insurance. He was a gifted and honest salesman. Three times he built his territory to a point that could comfortably support "his girls" (as he liked to call us in those preconscious times), and three times the company split his territory with two other men. The third time they did it, my dad brought in a union. But that is another story. As for my mom, she is one of the most instinctively justice-oriented people I know. She graduated with straight As from high school and dreamed of college, but that was rare for small-town women in the 1940s, and besides, there was a war on. She did get a scholarship to nursing school, however, and though she was unable to finish, her influence led my two cousins, my sister, and me to choose nursing over teaching, the two "respectable" options for women in the early 1960s. It was a given that my sisters and I would attend college or nursing school, though where the money would come from was less clear. To make ends meet, Mom got a job at the local Veteran's Office when my youngest sister entered first grade. Though it was hard, she loved her work because, being a very bright woman, she enjoyed the challenge. Mom's deep sympathy for the down-and-out was a major asset to many a struggling veteran, for whom she was a skillful advocate in a very bureaucratic system. My mother also had deep sympathy for the struggles of African American people, frequently lamenting over how unfair things were for them after listening to the news. One day, we discovered that an African American family was going to move in next door. Neighbors in our white, middle-class neighborhood were openly speculating about what my father would do. Dad, believing he had to protect his investment for "his girls," planned to move at the earliest possible opportunity. I can still hear my mother's vehement protest: "Paul Schenk, we've taught these kids all of our lives that black people are as good as we are. We are not going to change that now." Needless to say, we didn't move. The Ransoms proved to be among the nicest neighbors we'd ever had. No one else moved, either. My mom: the integrator. If the government had only been able to bottle the righteous indignation she exuded over racism, the 1960s would have been a whole lot sweeter.

I have been indignant about sexism in the Church ever since second grade, when they let Harry Miller be an altar boy but not me. I loved the ritual of the old Latin Mass, with its mystery, its bells, its muttered Latin phrases, while aromatic incense wafted lazily heavenward. Cherished childhood memories return—gilt-tinged plaster-of-Paris saints smiling beneficently at me, an all too earnest girl-child gazing raptly back. I just couldn't figure out how Harry Miller got to swing the incense when he wasn't nearly as smart or as well behaved as I was. I got straight As and the nuns doted on me. Being the oldest of my sisters, I was articulate, mature for my age, and had charming golden curls. I would have been a shoe-in for altar server in a less sexist world. Plus there was the problem that I wanted to be a priest. This had happened unexpectedly in second grade while attending daily Mass with crusty, old Father Fate (yes, it's his real name). I became acutely aware of the beauty and sacredness of the Mass, and of God. The thought came: "Oh, if only I were a boy, I would be a priest. But I can't; I'm a girl." I shoved this thought away, down deep inside. I never got over my love for the numinous, though I didn't know then how to name it, and still don't. In later years, I took comfort in the thought that though I was "only a girl," God didn't seem to mind, and frequently blessed me with experiences of reverence and love for the holy.

Faith in the Wasteland

But if I am to relate my whole life story, this will be a book and not a chapter in a book. I suppose my checkered history as a Catholic is the first abbreviation. Suffice it to say that I struggled through college (a miraculous scholarship to Georgetown University solved my money woes) in a dark night of the soul, wondering how there could possibly be a God with Vietnam, rampant racism, nuclear weapons, and D.C.'s 14th Street in flames after the assassination of Dr. Martin Luther King. Robert Kennedy was murdered three days before we graduated from college, taking with him any vestiges of idealism that remained for many in my generation. I was greatly supported in my faith crisis by a Jesuit priest, Fr. William Kaifer, who patiently met with me while I struggled with whether God existed. Somehow, I couldn't stand life if God didn't exist. On the other hand, who wanted to relate to the Yahweh-thunderbolt God of my childhood? All during this time, I continued to attend daily Mass. Even though I couldn't believe, it felt better to be around people who did. My Jesuit friend's love and faithfulness ultimately provided the heart-breakthrough experience I needed to image God as tenderly near—a *male* tenderly near, to be sure, but exponentially different from the God of my childhood. This God was also mysterious, creative and unpredictable. I began to love the Holy Spirit best of all of the persons of the Trinity. Jesus, I took for granted as my friend and the one who cared most about the poor and abandoned. My Jesuit friend, though a holy man and a loving father figure, opposed women priests, believing he was not to question whatever the Pope said. I remember thinking secretly to myself, "This is one thing that you are absolutely dead wrong about."

Oddly enough, the poet T.S. Eliot was also a great help. I studied his life and poetry and decided that if this great man of letters could finally come to belief after his devastating vision in *The Wasteland*, so could I. Teilhard de Chardin, the Jesuit paleontologist and mystic, provided the integration of faith and science I needed in those "God-is-dead" days of antipathy between science and religion. As I look back, I had few women heroes. Perhaps I took for granted the strong women in my life—both in my family and in my school world of nuns and nurses. The female literary, religious, and theological mentor-"heroes" were to arrive later, and not only in books.

Sexism, Sin, and the Catholic Church

The years after college were rocky but growthful. I met the seamy underside of ambition and negligence in the health care world. I also met some of the finest women on the planet, in the form of Medical Mission Sisters. I spent six formative years with them growing up and growing into what was to become my lifelong mission of advocacy for systemic justice in whatever system I happened to find myself. I was also gifted with my first female religious mentors, Sisters Estelle Demers, Kathryn Volker, Miriam Therese Winter, Margaret McKenna, Jane Burns, and others too numerous to name. These women loved, guided, and informed me, and challenged both my soul and my politics. I could no longer sustain my provincial corn-belt belief in "our U.S. Government right or wrong" after observing these strong missionary women returning from poorer nations of the world with real-life experience of the devastating effects of U.S. foreign policy.

I took a long reappraising look at the Catholic Church, heretofore an unexamined source of comfort and stability. I saw with fresh eyes the effects of Church politics as I heard true stories of bishops in foreign lands who demanded that the Sisters care only for the minuscule number of relatively well-to-do Catholics, leaving the majority of sick and suffering people to their own devices. But Mother Anna Dengel, the Society's founder, refused. After all, her founding call had been to bring health care to Muslim women in Pakistan who were dying by the thousands in childbirth. Purdah laws forbade male physicians to deliver their babies, and there were no female doctors to attend them. Mother Dengel was not about to abandon these women or their families. The Gospel called for an obedience different from the one the bishop thought he could demand.

I experienced first-hand as well the anger of the local hierarchy over the Sisters' innovative, prayerful liturgy that reflected their own life experiences. I saw how mean spirited this hierarchy could be with people who wouldn't march in lock step to a deadly dull drumbeat, choosing instead to dance to their own Spirit-inspired music, more often than not that of S. Miriam Therese Winter. Perhaps most revelatory was the visit of a simple sandal-shod bishop from India who came to the Sisters for an introduction to the reigning (and I do mean reigning) cardinal. The bishop was on a fund-raising mission for education resources for his growing number of seminarians. Though we tried to explain to him that Medical Mission Sisters were not exactly at the top of the cardinal's hit parade, Sister Margaret (whose last name will remain anonymous) agreed to accompany this gentle man to the chancery. The cardinal's palatial office afforded a stunning view of the city. Our Indian friend presented his needs humbly, only to hear the cardinal's brusque reply that he had nothing to give him. Despite rejection, our Indian bishop voiced no anger, resentment, or even criticism of the obvious wealth of the Archdiocese. This was hard to accept because even a small amount of money would have gone very far, given the huge number of rupees one could get for a dollar at the time. For a young nun, the disparities between the church of the first world and that of the developing world were all too obvious. This was the first time I seriously considered leaving the Catholic Church. Perhaps I would join the Quakers. They loved and understood silent prayer and were active justice and peace seekers. But in the end, I loved the Church too much to abandon it to its worst of its demons. I still feel that way.

Jesus, Justice, and Community Organizing

In 1973, after teaching nursing for a year, I became disgusted with what I experienced as academia's focus on ego-politics rather than teaching students. With the permission of my Medical Mission superiors, I took time off to work as the Interfaith Coordinator for the United Farm Workers Union (UFW) in Philadelphia's grape and lettuce boycott. At the time, many believed their cause was hopeless. Sixties' activism was rapidly on the wane, and the Teamsters Union was successfully signing sweetheart deals with growers who would do anything to keep Cesar Chavez out. Yet, because of skillful community organizing and the goodness of ordinary people who recognize a just cause when they see one, the UFW survives and thrives to this day. Unbeknownst to me, I was learning skills that would help me work for justice in other venues. Perhaps I could begin to do something about all those injustices that distressed my soul. In retrospect, all of the justice-causes for which I subsequently worked succeeded because of the organizing skills and the persevering spirit learned from the Farm Workers. I left Medical Mission Sisters in 1977, but a piece of my soul, and certainly my lifelong mission, remains linked to this remarkable community of global-justice-and-wholeness women. My own call was to be a more local ecclesial-justice one, and for this, the Cleveland Congregation of St. Joseph fit best. But that was later. For the time being, I was in deep confusion, not to say despair, because I felt abandoned by a God, whom I thought had called me into the sisterhood, and then inexplicably called me out. Recurrent depression was my reason for leaving, though the Sisters would have been glad had I stayed. I discovered six years later that a severe hypothyroid condition was the cause of my depressions.

In the meantime there were lessons to be learned in darkness that could never have been learned in lighter times. The first was of God's utter fidelity even in the midst of deep shadow. The second, introduced by a dear Baptist midwife-mentor, Elsie Maier Wilson, would be the most enlightening and revolutionary of my life. I returned to Eastern Kentucky, where I had studied to be a family nurse practitioner and a nurse midwife in preparation, or so I thought, for ministry in India as a medical missionary. With that dream dead, Elsie helped me begin to trust Jesus' power in my life more deeply than before. I had always loved and admired Jesus as a great lover of the poor, one who did not reject "the least of these." I also sensed from a very early age that if there was ever anyone on the side of the oppressed, it was Jesus. I did not know the Jesus whose personal care and intimate love was and is able to provide a healing and peace beyond understanding. It was this Jesus I came to know in the midst of my own despair. I learned to trust the One who had struggled mightily Himself. I also discovered a new "best friend" who was, for me, wise, witty, and ultimately compassionate.

On the systemic change front, I discovered that nurse practitioners were not permitted prescriptive authority in Kentucky. This threatened our work with poor women and their families in the remote mountains of Eastern Kentucky, a region with few physicians. We needed to change the law. We were warned that this would be a difficult, if not hopeless, task because of the power of the medical association and the pharmacy board. So began a year-long adventure of coalition building, educating, and organizing, which culminated successfully in changing the Nurse Practice Act to provide limited prescriptive authority for nurse practitioners. Many times as I was making the long drive to big-city Louisville from the remote simplicity of the mountains, I prayed for God's help to present our case well. Against all odds we succeeded because the common decency of ordinary Kentuckians recognized that the needs of their poorer mountain counterparts should take priority over petty interdisciplinary turf wars. But it was trust in Jesus' ability to empower the powerless, and the organizing skills learned from the Farm Workers, that gave me the courage to try. After a year of teaching and networking in Kentucky, I moved to Cleveland, where I became involved in two other systemic justice campaigns that provided invaluable experience for my future life's work of Church reform. The first was the sanctuary movement. The second was a statewide coalition, known as the Prenatal Investment Program (PNIP), which aimed to expand Medicaid to poor working mothers and their children.

Cleveland, Sanctuary, and Mothers and Babies

Clevelanders have a special sensitivity to the needs of Central America because two Salvadoran martyrs, Jean Donovan and

S. Dorothy Kazel, were from this Ohio city. In fact, both attended Mass at my own faith community, St. Malachi's. In 1984, the Community of St. Malachi began an eight-month discernment process about whether or not to grant sanctuary to political refugees fleeing torture and violent death in Central America. It was controversial, but the Community of St. Malachi eventually decided to place conscience over possible legal consequences and welcomed political refugees. In the succeeding four years, twenty-one Central American men, women, and children found refuge in our midst and, eventually, permanent legal residence in Canada. St. Malachi was one of three hundred sanctuary churches nationwide that, after a long legal struggle, finally forced what used to be known as the U.S. Immigration and Naturalization Services (INS—now part of the Bureau of Citizenship and Immigration Services [BCIS]) to abide by U.S. laws. As signers of the Geneva Accords and the Refugee Act of 1980, the United States is obligated to investigate each claimant's case for political asylum. Instead, the INS quickly deported political refugees without first investigating their claims of imminent injury or death if forced to return home. When we began, the obstacles seemed insurmountable. The INS was too intransigent, and what could only three hundred churches out of hundreds of thousands do in the face of such systemic blindness? As it turned out, quite a lot! After a protracted struggle, the sanctuary churches won their lawsuit and, today, Immigration Services must investigate each refugee's situation. The lesson here? A few just people can move mountains! Once again, the skills I learned from the Farm Workers served me well. We organized more than thirty prominent church and political leaders to publicly endorse our sanctuary position, long before the public prayer service welcoming "Pedro," our first sanctuary guest. This reduced our risk and created a wide safety net for us even as it broadened commitment to peace and justice in Central America. This grassroots base was very helpful later, when the Cleveland City Council declared Cleveland a Sanctuary City.

The second campaign arose from my work as a nurse midwife with low-income families in Cleveland's poorer neighborhoods. Due to "Reaganomics" we were struggling with cutbacks in health and nutritional programs that served poorer populations. Infant mortality rates in some Cleveland neighborhoods were higher than those in many developing countries. Hardest hit were working women too poor to have private insurance but making too much money to be on welfare. These women would show up in hospital emergency rooms in premature labor because they could not afford prenatal care. Too often their infants were born early, necessitating lengthy stays in neonatal intensive care units costing over thousands of dollars per day. All of this could be avoided with the far less expensive option of adequate prenatal care. It was very frustrating as a midwife to see babies not growing in the womb because their mothers didn't get enough to eat. Often this was because they would forego their own nutrition to feed other young children at home. Children whose diets had previously been supplemented by school lunch and WIC programs were now going hungry because of cuts by the Reagan administration. Of course, this administration was elected in part because of their so-called "pro-life" platform. Pro-life, that is, until the child is born; then it is apparently acceptable for her or him to go hungry.

With the Cleveland Commission on Catholic Community Action and the Cleveland Federation of Community Planning, I helped launch a statewide campaign to expand Medicaid to include low-income women and their children. Dubbed the "Prenatal Investment Program" (PNIP), we were once again told that our cause was well nigh impossible, given the cost-cutting legislative climate and the fiscal conservatism of the Ohio legislature (forty-seven other states had already passed legislation funding such a program). This became a five-year campaign with many ups and downs. Had I known what I was getting into, I'm not sure I would have proceeded. On the other hand, somebody had to do something, and it might as well have been me. We successfully established statewide grassroots coalitions in Columbus, Cincinnati, Toledo, and Dayton, as well as with many staunch supporters from Ohio's rural areas. Several Ohio politicians were especially helpful. Most influential was Representative Jane Campbell from Cleveland Heights, who at no small political risk guided PNIP through the legislature. It didn't hurt that Jane was pregnant with her first child at the time. She was an extraordinarily competent legislator who had a passion for the issue that only a mother can know. It was pretty hard for Jane's male counterparts to ignore this determined and powerful mother-to-be. To our delight, Governor Richard Celeste publicly supported us in his successful bid for re-election. Unfortunately, at the eleventh hour the Governor's senior staff betrayed us. Even though PNIP had been passed by both the Ohio House and Senate and had a modest budget, it was cut at the last minute. We were devastated, but quickly devised the best solution we could on short notice. We encouraged our statewide coalition to telephone Celeste's office and demand reinstatement. Over a two-hour period, more than one hundred and fifty calls flooded the Governor's office, successfully overwhelming and shutting down his telephone system. To the great chagrin of his staff, Governor Celeste capitulated. We were jubilant. Later, when people congratulated me on our come-from-behind victory, I replied: "Heck, if we had known it was going to work, we would have generated a thousand calls!"

FutureChurch Founding, Mission, and Vision

In 1986, I decided to follow my heart and return to the nunnery. After a period of discernment I knew that though I loved Medical Mission Sisters very much indeed, my call was not to health care in foreign missions. Locally, the Cleveland Congregation of St. Joseph was the group I admired most for their work empowering poor people and taking risks on behalf of justice. In 1990, I professed vows with them in a very joyful ceremony. That same year, the St. Malachi Community, in response to national Call to Action's "Call for Reform" initiative, asked me to co-chair a committee dealing with Church reform. Concurrently, a prophetic parish council at the Church of the Resurrection in Solon, Ohio, led by a holy and gifted priest, Fr. Louis J. Trivison, passed a resolution in response to a decision by the National Conference of Catholic Bishops to approve a communion rubric for Sunday worship in the absence of a priest. Their resolution said in part: "there is no lack of vocations to the ordained priesthood if we consider priests who have married and who are willing to lead the community in worship, married men who desire to be priests, and single and married women who feel called to the ordained priesthood." The parish council requested reconsideration of expanding ordination so as "to include women and men, married and single, so that the Eucharist may continue to be the center of the spiritual life of all Catholics." During the ensuing six years, a total of twenty-eight Catholic parishes and communities endorsed this resolution, which subsequently became FutureChurch's founding document.

The parishes' concerns were not misplaced. A study by demographers Richard Schoenherr and Lawrence Young, originally commissioned by the U.S. bishops themselves, had revealed a projected 40 percent decline in priests by the year 2005, compared to 1965 levels. To compound the problem, the number of Catholics was projected to increase by 65 percent. The St. Malachi and Resurrection activists joined forces and called a meeting of progressive Catholic leaders. On October 16, 1990, thirty-four representatives of sixteen faith communities met at St. Malachi, and the FutureChurch coalition was born. In keeping with basic principles of community organizing, we spent a year building our grassroots base before going public. The diocesan newspaper inadvertently spurred our organizing by publishing projections for Cleveland priests over the coming ten years. I have since come to appreciate deeply the leadership of the Cleveland diocese for refusing to keep the impending priest shortage a secret, as did so many other dioceses. In 1994, FutureChurch incorporated, and I became its first full-time director.

Seminary Surprises and Sorrows

As part of my own midlife evolution, I was simultaneously completing a second master's degree, this time in theology, from our local seminary. Enticed by a lifelong love of Scripture, I began attending classes part time while working as a midwife. I was surprised to find myself gradually shedding many preconceptions about Catholic theology. I discovered an academically challenging curriculum paired with wonderful modeling of pastoral behavior for priests-in-training. When I heard a classmate expressing what I saw as a stupid or naive opinion, my first instinct was to go for the jugular with facts and incisive argumentation. I would wait in vain for a similar response from my seminary teachers. Instead I witnessed their pastoral and respectful acceptance of the person, even while explaining the overlooked theological or biblical information needed to deal with the question. This was a very humbling experience. It also taught me how to deal with similar situations I would face in the future. I loved every bit of my experience at the seminary. I met women theologian mentors who provided both new insights into feminist theology and confidence in myself as a woman minister. More surprising to me were several priest mentors who encouraged and supported my budding ministerial skill. I graduated with a 4.0 grade point average, passed my comprehensive exams "with distinction," and was asked to preach at our graduation prayer service, which I did with joy and enthusiasm. My comprehensive work dealt primarily with the historical Jesus, women's roles in the first-century church, and the new Jesus movement rapidly growing. In 1993, it was still possible to study the theological and biblical arguments for and against women's priestly ordination. This formed yet another part of my comprehensive studies.

When ordination time came for my male classmates, I thought I would be okay. After all, just learning about scripture and theology was such an incredible gift, and God would know how to use my ministerial call. But it wasn't okay. It hurt far more than I had imagined to be excluded solely because of my gender. I knew with a certainty that filled my being that this was just devastatingly wrong. God had given me so much, but now I was to be silent and pretend that it hadn't happened? I thought of Catholic women the world over who are filled with the Spirit and a deep love of Scripture and of the Sacred who are also expected to be silent. And I was outraged at the arrogance of a structure that honestly believes it can silence the voice of God speaking and witnessing in and through female bodies. All of my life I had worked on behalf of "the oppressed," yet never until now was I fully able to own my own oppression as a woman in the Catholic Church. Like most oppressed peoples, it was too painful and felt too hopeless to consciously acknowledge. Yet now, I had a new set of tools, a new set of lessons to add to the organizing ones already in my repertoire. I knew beyond a shadow of a doubt that far from excluding women, Jesus had included and empowered them in a society even more brutally sexist than our own. He had done this to such an extent that first-century Christian women took for granted their leadership and prophetic roles, as reported in Paul's letter to the Romans (Romans 16). I realized as never before that Jesus was killed not because he was such a threat to the Roman overlords, but rather because he was a threat to his own religious leaders, who were in collusion with their oppression of the poor of the land. He was a threat because he would not be silent about a God who loves justice and truth in the heart above all. Jesus' God is an unpredictable and uncontrollable mystery whose ultimate compassion and tenderness provided the "Jesus Way" so that human frailty and sin do not have the final word. This God raised Jesus from the dead and sent women as the first witnesses in a system that did not even recognize them as legal witnesses. Though their society discounted them, God did not. If the religious leadership had accepted Jesus' standards of holiness, they would have had to change their own lives to ones of "downward mobility" on behalf of the "least ones" who were Jesus' special care. They were not about to do that, so obviously, Jesus had to go. Women know very well about being the "least ones." They know from their own experience what it is to be discounted, excluded, and made invisible. This truth alone gives many of us a powerfully personal understanding of the Jesus message and a powerful gift of preaching from our experience. What a potent energy for justice among the nations and among people would be released were women given equal opportunity with their brothers to preach the Gospel. In reality, I wonder if this is the possibly unconscious but real reason women are forced to be silent in Catholic churches. Is it because too many of us don't want to be challenged on behalf of the excluded? Or is it simply that the male celibate power structure can't stand a little healthy competition? The parallels with Jesus' confrontation of the religious power structure of his day seem all too obvious.

It's Always Darkest before the Dawn: Ordinatio Sacerdotalis and the Dubious Dubium

No sooner had I opened our first official FutureChurch office in 1994 than Pope John Paul II issued *Ordinatio Sacerdotalis* (*OS*), the opinion that Church teaching about the non-ordination of women was definitive, could not be changed, and was therefore not to be talked about, studied, or discussed. This was followed eighteen months later (apparently to stop the intensified talk, study, and discussion) by the *Responsum ad Dubium*. This second document from the Congregation of the Doctrine of the Faith offered the opinion that the teaching on the non-ordination of women could even be considered infallible. I promptly dubbed the *Responsum ad Dubium* the "dubious Dubium" because, according to canon law, only the Pope can issue infallible documents, not Vatican offices, no matter how much Papal approbation they invoke. It was a pretty sleazy move by people who should have known better. In May of 1997, after a year-long study, the Catholic Theological Society of America voted by an overwhelming majority to approve a document demonstrating that the teaching on the non-ordination of women could not be considered to be infallible and, in fact, should continue to be studied and discussed. In the meantime, the pressure to keep quiet about women's equality issues in the Church reached new levels of intensity. Women ministers were afraid to even talk with each other about the shock they felt over the extreme measure of attaching the word "infallible" to women's ordination. This fear was intensified in Cleveland because our bishop, Anthony Pilla, had just been installed as president of the National Conference of Catholic Bishops. He received the document from Rome not five hours after his installation, a most inauspicious way to begin his tenure, to say the least. One had to wonder about the timing. It was very, very difficult to not feel betrayed after reading the bishop's obligatory prelude to the

Vatican document, asking everyone in the U.S. Church to accept it. To his credit he never used the word "infallible" in his introductory letter. When he came home, he let it be known that he wanted to establish dialogue with female diocesan leaders about the pastoral fallout from this ill-advised document. The fear factor diminished considerably, and people began to discreetly air their feelings. Nevertheless, it was hard not to lump our own bishop in with all of the other oppressive male hierarchical figures. I couldn't quite do this, however, because I knew him to be very supportive of women in leadership. Though unwilling to take a public stand, he appointed women to very responsible positions in the diocese with minimal fanfare.

With this latest salvo from the Vatican, not only did I counsel women wondering how they could remain in the Church with integrity, I also counseled several priests anguishing over how they could continue to publicly represent an institution with such clearly sexist, if not repressive, policies and teachings. Their fear was even more palpable in some instances than that of women ministers. I listened and then suggested that their inclusive, women-friendly ministry was needed now more than ever. I also connected several justice-minded priests with each other for mutual support. It was oddly consoling to me to realize that some of my brothers were in anguish over these divisive and destructive teachings. Misery loves company I guess, and that this misery crossed gender boundaries was a hopeful, if painful, sign of solidarity.

I also began to experience rejection by individuals and groups in both the local and national scenes. Conservative protesters appeared at presentations I gave on the priest shortage, accusing me of disloyalty to the Pope, heresy, denying the real presence of Christ in the Eucharist, being a bad nun, and assorted other infractions such as not wearing a habit. Thinly veiled personal criticisms appeared in both diocesan and secular newspapers. Ultra-conservative publications such as *The Wanderer* and *Crisis* magazines wrote articles falsely quoting me, using language not remotely in my repertoire. Closer to home, the diocese received a request from Rome inquiring why I had earlier been granted certification as a pastoral minister. There was pressure from local church officials to hold our FutureChurch programs on non-Catholic property. When I began traveling more widely, reactions were mixed. Some dioceses publicized my presentations in their newspapers, and some chancery officials even shared their most recent priest shortage statistics. Other dioceses banned my presentations altogether and denied that the priest shortage affected them at all. They preferred to ignore the messenger rather than face a future with very few priests. None of this really bothered my soul too much. I had been involved in too many systemic change movements in the past not to know that some persecution simply goes with the territory. Such extreme efforts on the part of prevailing power structures are actually hopeful signs. The energies for change must be getting much stronger and more significant. Why else launch such vigorous resistance? Rather than cause for despair, *OS* and the *Responsum* were cause for optimism. Vatican statements on the non-ordination of women could be speeding up the process leading to their eventual ordination even more than we had dared to hope. I was comforted by the thought that Paul the Apostle had been thrown out of all the best synagogues in the known world for preaching that belief in Jesus Christ, not circumcision laws, was what put one right with God. I was in very good company.

Balm in Gilead

While there have been painful, doubt-filled times, there have also been grace, consolation, and support in abundance. I have received a great deal of affirmation from my religious community, the Congregation of St. Joseph (CSJ). With its long history of peace activism, advocacy for ending U.S. funding of wars in Central America, and support for homeless women, my community is accustomed to justice struggles. There was never any question of being asked to stop my work for church reform, despite its potential risks. This is an extraordinarily great gift, which I probably too often take for granted. My CSJ spiritual director at the time kept me grounded in the fact that "You are not the only tree giving shade in this forest." This turned out to be a great mantra for someone with a messiah complex as big as mine. My Medical Mission friends had a remarkable knack for sending just the right card at just the right time. I could never have survived without the nurturing of all of my sisters, who perhaps know better than anyone what it takes to do this work.

Jesus

It is through community support and worship that we relive the dangerous memory of Jesus, who knew well how to love his faith community despite rejection. He loved it fiercely, even though many could only return that love with hatred. Jesus' love was patient, nonviolent, and essential to building strong communities. These communities then went on to love both God and neighbor greatly, since these are inseparable in Jesus' eyes. This God-love evokes just actions and truth in the heart. It is the compassionate love of a prodigal Father who did not uphold patriarchal norms but instead welcomed a wayward boy-child home with joy and celebration. It is the passionate and compassionate love of the wise Sophia-Spirit whose mighty strength led Jesus first to the desert and then supported and nurtured him even to the laying down of his life rather than compromise a lifelong witness to a God of love and of justice. Mary of Magdala, Joanna, Salome, and Mary were the first to experience this same God's loving response to Jesus' fidelity-unto-death. Inexplicably, God raised Jesus from death to new life. Now, all of us would finally be able to see, understand, and begin to experience *this extraordinarily powerful love* that is able to deal with death and evil and sexism and fear and hatred. Jesus' powerful risen love overcomes all of these. With the help of his wise Sophia-Spirit, so shall we.

Part Three

The Holy Spirit Confirms

& The Truth Shall Set U Free

Jane Morrissey

"(Un)Ruly . . . ?"
Who says?
Who sets the rules?
Puts in parentheses?
Chooses capitals?
The Church of Trent
Or Vatican I
Or Vatican II
Or *the* Vatican

Or those who stand up
Up
Up
For the Gospel
And are willing to lay down their lives for just that

Or a little of all this and more:

Responding to the signs of the times
From the margins
Of the newsprint

And the neighborhood
And the barrio
And protesting
The wings of whatever drones
Come in surveillance with instruments of violence?

Who says?
I ask
From where I sit
At the computer
Composed and composing
In a gray house
To which I was called
By to Whom it does concern?

By that very church
That called Action
On behalf of Justice
A constituent element
Of Evangelization

And that coined the phrase
That falls not so easily
Out of a human heart
As it does out of the blood
Of those who mean it?
Yes.
Turn toward the poorest of the poor
And the youngest of the young
For whom there is declared
A preferential option,

For of such is heaven made
Says the One in whom we believe
And it is at hand
If we don't mind getting fingernails dirty
And feet smelling like sheep.

I suspect
That very Pontifical Church
That caught and taught me
As a child and adolescent and Sister of Saint Joseph
Taught me unawares to be (Un)Ruly.
This is that part of my story
It's how, when, where, and why
As far as I can figure.

Once upon a time
In 1976
I got the letters PhD after my name, now Jane F. Morrissey, SSJ,
After nine years of study
Including some months
Working with early Advent Vespers manuscripts on microfiche
At the Pontifical Institute of Mediaeval Studies
In Toronto.

Under a heavy yoke
Of obedience to a Leadership Team
That denied me permission to teach at Pine Ridge Reservation,
I went to teach at our College of Our Lady of the Elms
In Chicopee, Massachusetts,
And was granted a permission
To live off campus in a poor neighborhood nearby
That lessened the weight of that yoke some.

That permission
Became the gate through which S. Mary Dooley
Congregational president through
The Post-Vatican Extraordinary Chapter
Released me
To engage in post-doctoral study called *la vida* in the unruly
World of the North End of Springfield, Massachusetts.

Mary did understand
And stand for something new.

Through the 1970s she was working with Sisters Joan Chittister,
Joan Doyle, and Theresa Kane
At unruly LCWR,
Leadership Conference of Women Religious yet under the
Vatican microscope.
It was she who had introduced me to the "Church in the Mod-
ern World"
And other documents written by the *periti*
She met when earning her PhD at the Sorbonne
Where she had heard the sixties' protest in Paris,
"Be reasonable. Do the impossible."
In the seventies she flew on Air Force I with Vice President Walter
Mondale
To the installations of John Paul I and II.

It was she who said, in the tumult of change when I was
penned up
At our motherhouse without newspapers, that
We young nuns should show up and pay attention to the
Catholic Peace Fellowship
Gathering from our New England states at Mont Marie.
By then keynote speaker Gordon Zahn had uncovered
Brave Austrian Franz Jägerstätter *In Solitary Witness.*
Late that morning
Of the Fellowship gathering
Someone in blue jeans told me
To get in line.

In some cloud of unknowing I left Mont Marie with strangers
In a stranger's van
And stood uncomfortably in protest
At a Holyoke market selling Gallo Wine.

All right. I would teach at the Elms by day
And live among the poor by night,
And see outside of school *el barrio de mi vida.*
Christmas vacation taught me how

Homeless huddled in the basement laundry
Near dryers, their fireside;
I began to understand
What it is to live between fear
And love on Sheldon Street
And share my struggle
In prayer with the One Who matters more
And more.

Vatican II seeped into my Modern World,
With the anxieties and joys of the people of our times,
Especially the poor. Along the few miles
I walked through the North End toward the College, I began
    to feel
Interfaith. On my way to Father Dan Shea's seven o'clock
    Mass
I often met a Jewish wanderer of the age I've now reached
Who would confide in me memories savored while crossing the
    city from Forest Park.
It was a Martin Buber time: he'd tell me the history of our
    neighborhood where
The lights of his synagogue's Star of David
In this decade
Greeted the Spanish Assembly of God.

Kathy and I did the work of Church
In Blessed Sacrament Parish
Where we found ourselves
On the way
That enlarged the meaning of home
And started reaching toward the America of the Southern
    Hemisphere.

When Kathy and I asked the pastor
On the feast of Saint Therese for whom he had a shrine
And novena, if we might be of help to him,
Father Dan's mouth opened wide and

Let us in on his few remaining yellowing teeth.
He inquired if we were allergic to CCD.
He was then teaching kindergarten to eighth
And snow blowing the parking lot and sidewalks
And assembling retired and active police
Every morning for coffee and doughnuts,
While hanging for dear life on what he learned from his
    Church as
"Objective truth."

We took on middle school,
Met children lagging in reading,
And my mother came from Westfield
Once a week to teach them, as she had me.
God cared too,
As did Father Dan poaching eggs to serve us after morning Mass.

We lived in the block
Owned by Jack and Mollie O'Shea
Who, upon hearing that we wouldn't, couldn't in conscience
    pay
More than the 110 dollars calculated for two Sisters in a
    convent
For one month's rent,
Responded that so long as we would pray for
What we couldn't pay for,
They'd not lose a cent having us as their tenants.

One night Father Shea had us for dinner
And decorated the dining room with Gallo wine posters
From his friends' Table and Vine.
He protested when
In solidarity with Cesar Chavez and the United Farmworkers
We wouldn't drink the wine his housekeeper served.
For dessert he and the bakery produced a cake iced with the
    name of Kathy's workplace.

At WRAP, Westfield Resource Action Planning, she worked with
    troubled adolescents.
In blue icing he let us know what he suspected:
"Women Ruin Apostolic Priesthood."

I was learning to be a woman religious on many levels.
Through the 1974 merger of the Fall River Province of the
    first
Daughters of Saint Joseph with our diocesan group,
I was hearing from them stories of our earliest history.
Little Sister Emma Boivin stood up to tell us how in 1650
Our Sisters divided their village into quarters,
Walked the streets by day, and by night
Prayed over what they saw
To discern what they were to do
"That all may be one."
Why not try that in our barrio?

Change the Church in the Modern World?
Reading the NCR in our third-floor apartment,
I remember thinking it nervy of me
To entertain questions about nuclear power
If I hadn't studied physics
Since junior year of high school,
Until Sam Lovejoy took a crowbar
To the tower for the proposed plant
In Montague just north of us
And helped me hear my conscience
Instructing me
Otherwise in truth beyond
Einstein's formulas.

I began feeling the ferment
Of Puebla and Medellin over the phone when Father Bernie Survil
Called out of the blue, on the recommendation
Of Mike True of the Catholic Peace Fellowship,

To ask that we arrange a lecture at the Elms College and Mont
    Marie
On the crisis in Guatemala and, dumb, I asked
"Where is that country?"

When the 1980s dawned
In the North End, we were becoming a community
Of six—Cathy, Eileen, Julie, Joan, Kathy, and me—five Sisters
And our Baptist neighbor.

The three-story hundred-year-old gray house
Two doors down from Jack and Mollie's block
Had stood empty since the month Kathy and I moved
To Sheldon Street and
A cigarette butt left a charred gaping hole in the living room
    ceiling.
Our interest opened the door to a place where a tree was growing
In the first-floor bathtub.

With permission
We bought that seventeen-room house for five hundred dollars
    in 1982
And went to work with everyone we knew
And many we didn't. With the help of neighbors, pre-release
    prisoners, guards,
Girl Scouts, Elms students and alumnae, our Sisters, families,
    and friends,
Under the direction of the North End's Hallahan Lumber,
That Gray House began teaching us that
Deference needs a measure of defiance in order to
Open ourselves to change.

Sacred memory in active prayer began to connect us
Across the Americas with Romero
And our courageous Sister women religious—Jean, Ita, Maura,
    and Dorothy—
Martyred in El Salvador.
CISPES enabled us to work for justice here and there.

Then with her unruly integrity
Penny Lernoux came to speak at the Elms on Human Rights in
    Latin America
And stayed with us at the Gray House.
She said, as does *el pueblo de nuestro barrio,* "Mi casa es tu
    casa."
In response I went with students to her house in Bogotá.
Then and there I learned what a snob I can be
After saying to a woman in a homeless shelter
Hunched over an indecipherable paper
That I couldn't read her writing.
Humbled to tears I listened as staff explained what a struggle it
    was for her
To dare hold a writing instrument.

I heard another's voice asking His followers
"Are you yet without understanding?"

Penny came and came back.
I began going back and forth to South America.
She gave our commencement address
When the Elms awarded her an honorary degree.

She says, "You can look at a slum or peasant village,
but it is only by entering into that world—by living in it—that
you begin to understand what it is like to be powerless,
to be like Christ."

She helped me discern
What my commitment to Gospel nonviolence meant
After unsuccessfully protesting the incorporation
Of ROTC for nursing students at the College
That had taught me
To love Dorothy Day and peace.

In the fall of 1989, Penny died shortly after
She learned she had cancer. A month later
At the University of San Salvador, six Jesuits,

Their housekeeper, and her teen-aged daughter,
Were massacred by graduates of the Georgia-based
School of the Americas.

A month later I left
The North End of Springfield
With Maureen Broughan, SSJ, for a few weeks in Central
    America,
Studying Spanish in Antigua, Guatemala,
I began praying unawares
To Hermano Pedro de San Jose Betancur
At the hole in the wall of the Franciscan Church
That held his bones.

The following September I left the Elms to work again at Mont
    Marie
Staffing our SSJ Office for Justice and Peace. No sooner
Did I open the Office, when the first Bush President started
Rumbling toward the first, now our prolonged, War in Iraq.
Some members of our Gray House community had begun to
    leave our home
For study and new lives. An aspirant to our life in the Sisters of
    Saint Joseph
Spoke up at the kitchen table. Annette speculated
That if she were I, she would have to risk arrest in protest. The
    hypothesis
Went clunk in my heart. She did nonviolence training with me.

On the eve of Martin Luther King Day,
Snow covered the ground at the gates of Westover Air Force
    Base and
I was taken by van to the Chicopee Police Station.

The previous time I was allowed into a basement lockup,
I had pigtails and braces shining on my teeth.
Teaching her seventh-graders the Baltimore Catechism
Lesson on the Corporal Works of Mercy,

Sister Joseph Paul assigned us to live them, not just recite them,
And turn in an essay
After doing one we'd never done before. My attorney father
Took me to visit the imprisoned. He introduced me to Romeo
On the other side of the bars,
A wandering alcoholic who used to sleep in the playground just
    blocks from our house,
Down by the dike. After our brief but unforgettable visit, my
    father told me
That in inclement weather the Westfield police would stand at
    the top of the dike
And holler, "Romeo, Romeo, where art thou, Romeo,"
And bring him to their one cell for a hot meal and dry sleep.

Since studying the Catechism
And the documents of Vatican II
I had begun reading Gandhi
And recognizing my silent complicity in the evil of my time.
It was Martin Luther King Day, 1991.
I was convinced that nonviolent love is the beating heart
Of the Gospel incarnated in Jesus the Christ
And taught truly and beautifully in the challenge of Beatitudes
I had also memorized from the Baltimore Catechism.
I remain convinced that only organized active nonviolent love
Has the power to undo evil.
Yet what was I doing in my Office for Justice and Peace?

About seventy of us stood in a circle
In the Station basement.
Slowly everyone joined the Taize Chant,
"Ubi caritas et amor
Ubi caritas, Deus ibi est."
Where there is love, there is God.
God is there.

Among those seventy-plus arrested were a Sister of Notre Dame
    and I.

Hattie, the seasoned protest organizer and a good Jewish mother
From the Buddhist Peace Pagoda,
Asked us two to be the last processed. We agreed.
She somehow believed we two Sisters had the power to stay any
    hand raised in violence.
As the last, we three were locked up with the one juvenile, a
    Quaker high school student
From Providence, in a broom closet with shelves doubling as
    our beds.

The courts decided to leave our arrest on the books
"Without a finding." In February I went to the gates again
Wearing a black scarf in solidarity with the grieving women of Iraq
And was remanded to the same court file.

My work in the Office for Justice and Peace was
Coupled with continuing study of languages in Guatemala.
I had wanted to converse more effectively with my neighbors.
Some grace had seized me
When my heart leapt out of my body
Before the interred bones of Hermano Pedro de San Jose Betancur.
I felt impelled to learn more Spanish and an indigenous lan-
    guage, Kaqchikel,
So that I could collect stories
From both Mayan and Ladino narrators
With Cristina Canales,
My Cuban colleague at the Elms.

We went back and forth for five years,
Finding the people who told the stories
For the 1996 trilingual publication,
Gracias, Matiox, Thanks, Hermano Pedro,
The unlikely consequence of my doctoral studies in oral tradition.

My time in Guatemala
Exposed me directly to injustice across the Americas originating
    in my native land.
I began protesting at the School of the Americas.

I also began dreaming of doing mission work
Somewhere south of the U.S. border,
But, becoming more involved in our Gray House neighborhood,
My dreams of mission brought me instead more deeply to
    where I am.

When something in me wanted to tell him that he belonged in
    Peru,
Peruvian Padre Juan, now our pastor, told me I belong here.
He was right. Penny Lernoux was right.
She often said that the violence we are responsible for in Latin
    America
Would return to our soil and haunt us.
Violence escalated in the North End.

I began working in my parish,
The same Blessed Sacrament where I had met Father Dan Shea,
But with a different congregation praying together more often
    in Spanish than English. My first week as pastoral assistant,
    we buried both a sixteen-year-old boy,
Whose sister's murder at fourteen in Hartford had occasioned
    the family's move here,
And the twenty-one-year-old mother of two.

Fathers Juan and Michael blessed me
When I went to the gates of the SOA,
Originally named the School of the Americas and
Dubbed by protesters School of Assassins,
Committed to risking my third arrest at those gates,
Aware that I was also risking five years in prison
By violating the Ban and Bar order I had earned
By my two previous arrests.

Of the founders of the Gray House
S. Cathy Homrok and I remained.
She and Annette, whose hypothesis initiated the discernment for
    my first arrest,

Offered to accompany me. S. Carol, then working for the local
   District Attorney,
Joined us as our Sister most familiar with courts.
We arrived at our motel near the base to a phone message
That saddened us on many levels.
Michael, our pastor, collapsed, was hospitalized, and might not
   survive.
What was there to do but continue discerning?
Always the unruly question:
What is the more loving thing to do?

I did not risk arrest. We walked and chanted and witnessed and
   came home.
Then as the millennium closed and I once more discerned
Defying the Ban and Bar Order and risking arrest,
I was elected President of the Sisters of Saint Joseph of Springfield.

While serving as president, trapped between internal and exter-
   nal responsibility
And alert to the primary call of conscience,
I knew anew and at new depth
That staple of American poetry I often dismiss as oversimplified
   and overused.
The rarely quoted stanza of Robert Frost's "The Road Not Taken"
   reminds us:

>   And both that morning equally lay
>   In leaves no step had trodden black.
>   Oh, I kept the first for another day!
>   Yet knowing how way leads on to way
>   I doubted if I should ever come back.

When the second President Bush started escalating
The call for war in Iraq, I went to Washington
In new shoes as President, and
In the name of the community,
When war broke, I knew not what to do until the day arrived

When I asked our Leadership Team—Maureen, Cathy, Patty, and
    Fran—
If they would support me.
They said yes and encouraged me to ask the entire community
And 90 percent of my Sisters said yes,
And, after breaking bread,
On the day U.S. troops entered Baghdad,
I was arrested
In front of the Federal Building in Springfield.

Many of the arresting officers had been my students
In the 1990s
During a one-semester stint teaching
"The Gospel Imperative for Justice and Peace"
In Anna Maria College's Criminal Justice Program.
One of those officers persuaded the matron
To serve us supper. For the first time since elementary school,
I ate bologna on Dreikorn's white sandwich bread.
Our cells were cold, but we were singing in parts.

This time the case went to trial.
A Quaker lawyer from Northampton offered his services;
I became the spokesperson for the band of arrestees.
We learned from films viewed by the Judge
That National Security posted armed agents
On the roofs of the buildings surrounding us
In downtown Springfield as the snow gracefully flurried on our
    shoulders.
We had resisted orders. We had continued to kneel and pray.

When I spoke before the Judge that day, I quoted the Preamble
To the Constitution which I had memorized as the consequence
Of some classroom misbehavior in Sister Joseph Paul's Seventh
    Grade
At St. Mary's School. Richard, my lawyer brother,
Advised me to include in our defense reference

to Article XIV of our Massachusetts Constitution
Granting freedom and rights to citizens for expressing legitimate
grievance.
We were found "Not guilty."

The finding echoed a conversation I had
The morning after this arrest
At Mont Marie Health Care Center
At the bedside of my Directress of Novices,
Sister Helen Benard.
"Jane," said she, looking at me solemnly,
"I saw the morning paper. Were it not for my condition,
I would have been at your side."

For the 350th anniversary of the 1650 founding of the Sisters
of Saint Joseph,
Our Leadership Team walked in the Holyoke St. Patrick's Day
Parade.

We mark our founding as the day when six women,
Under the guidance of a Jesuit priest thought maverick by his
community
For working with our sex,
Signed their vows. Only one could write her name.
On the parade route, S. Maureen, whose plans inspired my
involvement in Guatemala,
Noticed that in that city of Holyoke, the sixth poorest in the
U.S.,
Home to our Mont Marie Motherhouse,
Cheers greeted our contingent except in the poor minority
neighborhoods.
After that day, she and I wondered and prayed about
What we would do next.

As I write, I look back on the nine years since
Completing a term of Congregational Leadership.
We founded Homework House where
We have served Holyoke elementary school children

In those very neighborhoods where once no one knew our name
Or calling.

The community in our U.S. Federation
In Orange, California, especially Nancy O'Connor, Bridget
    Murphy, and Mary Madaleva,
Inspired us to do what two friends, Barbara Abouchar and
    Marcia Marcinko,
Did on the West coast from the Church of Mary Magdalen near
    their motherhouse.

We started with two third-graders named Jose
And two tutors from the Elms, Veronica and Jessie.
Now Monday through Thursday, a hundred or so come
And twice their number come to tutor. We named the program
    officially
The Homework House of Hermano Pedro
After now canonized Santo Hermano Pedro of Guatemala.
Whenever desperate for help,
We turn to him and have not been disappointed.
Even before tutoring started, Maureen and I were surprised to
    find his statue
On the altar at the Church in the Flats that offered us room.
She commented aloud, "You got here before we did."

Children are life to me now. When I started this journey,
Childhood was over my shoulder. Now I hobble down the stairs
When children from down the street
Near the Gray House ring the doorbell
And tell me their stories and dreams
Or look for a cookie or baseball. I'm glad when Deirdre,
The youngest in our community of four,
Gets to the door before me.

Programs go on under our Gray House apartment,
Much as they have from the beginning, food for body and mind
    and spirit,
For those giving and receiving.

At breakfast one sunny summer morning,
Cathy's voice alerted me to something more significant
Than the news, comics, sports, and obituaries she often high-
lights for me.
The lead editorial in the *Springfield Sunday Republican* took us
by surprise,
Telling our thirty-year story.
It quoted an anonymous synopsis of our dream from thirty years
ago:

> Our general purpose is most clearly stated in Gospel terms.
> We want to restore the Gray House as a place in which
> we can love others
> as Christ has loved us and help them to love one another.
> We sincerely believe that the life of nonviolent love
> is the only viable alternative to the tension and violence
> that now too frequently characterize life in our neigh-
> borhood.

State Representative Cheryl A. Coakley-Rivera concludes the
editorial, noting

> Gray House took an essentially forgotten zone of the
> North End and
> stabilized it . . . It's like your mom's house—
> you can go there for anything:
> food, company, a sweater.

In the second decade of life as Sister Jane,
The UnRuly life I yet enjoy began with its own brand of half-
blind obedience.
It led me to a neighborhood
That introduced me to a world I would not otherwise know.
The more I learned,
The further I went into the Church in the Modern World. In this
Gray House at dawn

We sit quietly in the turret,
Listen to the Word of God,
Share prayer,
And the sun rises.
We go out and do what we do.
At the close of the day,
We pray, sleep, and dream toward tomorrow.

Sisters behind Walls

Paula Timpson

Sisters behind walls
Share prayers with the Lord
They trust in Jesus
More than anything
Quietly miracles unfold
Creating mystery and curiosity
Of outsiders and people
In need of healing light
Sisters behind walls dance
With the Lord
In intimacy and courage
Not ever alone they sit with the
Blessed Sacrament
Aware of the needs of others
Outside the walls are they free
Or in the company of evil
Can sisters come out
Live and show their shiny eyes
Glowing faces
Hearts on fire
For
God

Rose Hawthorne Creates

Liz Dolan

Unlike my father, Nathaniel's, words,
mine scuttled like tangled limbs

on the page until a cancerous seamstress,
leaven for rats in an East Eleventh gutter,

stirred my muse. Before she was quarantined
on Blackwell's Island, I cleansed pus

from her stippled scabs, dripped honey
on her blistered lips, lay her rotting shell

on soft white sheets. Her breath's last vibration,
a vine of ivy I wove into grace which spun

my work of solace into breathless prose.

Note

Rose Hawthorne was the founder of the Dominican Sisters of the Sick
Poor.

When Grief Opens the Doors
to the Sacred

Michele Birch-Conery

From a Memorial Service presided by Reverend Doctor Michele Birch Conery and Reverend Doctor Barbara Billey, Co-pastors, Heart of Compassion International Inclusive Faith Community

WHEN GRIEF OPENS THE DOORS TO THE SACRED,
we come to the thinning seasons, summer to Autumn and then
     to winter
when eternity enters our awareness keenly. We diminish,
     somewhat, within the great spaces
of our universe, while parts of our planet enter a resting and
     dying time a fallow time to
prepare, without apology, the renewals of Spring.
Our dying, at any time of year, is like this. It is as if we could
     see
Through to and reach into eternity, even as our bodies
     surrender
To their necessities and then weaken toward the moments
Of their last breathing. We are held and embraced by
     spaciousness
Beyond ourselves. It is a time we are slowly coming to know

Though, yes, this could happen in a flash. We could be taken
As if by lightning, a sudden blizzard, a flood of something
We couldn't name.

They said, "She loved greatly and always. For this she was
    dearly loved."
They said, "We were always together, three sisters a year apart
    in age,
and now the very fabric of ourselves is torn." She said. "I
    built a dream home deep in nature and we have immersed
    ourselves in its joy."
She said, "It is yours now. You are dearly loved here."

He said, "She loved us dearly here and she was dearly loved."
    Three years and then
our living, our loving place became the place of her dying.
I was with her, always, in the ravaging of her cancer.
They said, "Every day she sat before her windows. She observed
    her world
for hours, and often we sat and observed with her.
Everything became quiet. We were deeply loved."

We said. "Their grief is profound. It feels impenetrable.
Let us hold it as our mothering God
holds it. We ask our God to hold their grief
in the infinity of her compassionate embrace."
And then? Art expression and poetry came to us.

A Woman
sits before her living
room window.
Long and wide
the window reflects
vistas of green

against a cloudless sky
where eagle and hawk
drift in easeful flight.

Their motionless wings
reflect on the wall behind her,
while the wall casts out shapes

that hang in the trees.
Inside out, outside in
she is drawn

toward the great
universe that has come
to meet her.

She receives everything
given. She gives all
she has ever received.

She greets the immense
surrounding space
she has sought

all her life. The reality
of surround space
is an embrace that

she now knows
is a gift
of loving presence.

A woman sits
before her
backyard window.

Long and wide,
the window reflects
stands of White Spruce,

Trembling Aspen.
Closer to her garden, to her patio,
she sees her flourishing

Dogwood, her Shining Willow.
Closer yet comes her cherished
Wilderness Rose, her Mountain Holly.

The window brings in myriad colors,
From her vegetable garden
protected by Firethorn, Blackthorn,

and her Fuchsia colored Gooseberry.

The window casts a vision of Paradise
on the wall behind her
while the wall returns images

of stained glass vases, golden spheres,
crystal gems that hang from the ceiling.
They fill the trees and the sky

as far as she can see.
On the surface of the glassed-in patio door
she sees how thin she has become.

A yellow color dots her nose
as if it had been kissed by a buttercup.
She sees that the yellow pervades her face

and neck. She sees that her hands are becoming
almost Autumn orange and brown
just like the markings on the leaves

drying a bit at the edges
of her cherished trees.
Every day she sits here,

her favorite quilt
wrapping her knees and her feet.
She needs this warmth now

in the thinning,
deepening season.
Questions arise within her.

She accepts them while
allowing them to quietly
find their place. Now she enters

the inner sanctuary of her heart.

Outside in, inside out,
the vast universe
claims her further than

she has ever been.

This is not a strange place.
She sees she is again
in a vast surrounding space

so organically lush
she cannot resist
its seductions.

All her life she attended
her beautiful world,
the one given to her and the one she created.

She knows she is entering it now.
Her fulfillment is at hand.
She will be home always

where home has always been, inside and out,
outside and in, there is no difference.
The reality

of surrounding space
is an embrace,
a kiss of peace, a welcome

she now knows
is a gift
of loving presence.

Notes on Contributors

Michele Birch-Conery has a lifetime of unruly examples, instances of creative acts taking her past the edges of the known and familiar, then staying with the tensions there. Staying and breathing and finding the ecstasy of it, then bringing it into expression, telling it as she is doing now. She sees the child with messy hair despite her finely pressed ribbons, so much not quite fitting but, oh, the rightness of expression always. She serves as a Bishop in the Association of Roman Catholic Women Priests and lives in Windsor, Ontario, today in this greening season, seeing it luminous in our surrounding space.

Ann Breslin was born in Derry, Ireland, in 1964. She has master's degrees in both education and religious studies, the latter with distinction. She develops and delivers retreats and courses centered on releasing the transformative power of story by reclaiming and retelling stories that connect us to our spirituality. Ann was one of the subjects of an award-winning documentary series called Beyond Belief. She is currently preparing the launch of Soulwais, a website and blog dedicated to recovering what has been distorted in the name of religion and discovering the ability to change, to begin again.

Jeana DelRosso is Professor of English and Women's Studies and director of the honors program at Notre Dame of Maryland

University in Baltimore. She is the author of *Writing Catholic Women: Contemporary International Catholic Girlhood Narratives* (Palgrave MacMillan, 2005). She is co-editor with Leigh Eicke and Ana Kothe of *The Catholic Church and Unruly Women Writers: Critical Essays* (Palgrave MacMillan, 2007) and *Unruly Catholic Women Writers: Creative Responses to Catholicism* (SUNY Press, 2013). Her articles have appeared in books as well as in such journals as *NWSA Journal, MELUS,* and *The Journal of Popular Culture.*

Liz Dolan's poetry manuscript, *A Secret of Long Life,* nominated for both the Robert McGovern Prize, Ashville University, and a Pushcart, has been published by Cave Moon Press. Her first poetry collection, *They Abide,* was published by March Street. A nine-time Pushcart nominee and winner of Best of the Web, she was a finalist for Best of the Net 2014. She won The Nassau Prize for Nonfiction, 2011, and the same prize for fiction, 2015. She has received fellowships from the Delaware Division of the Arts, The Atlantic Center for the Arts, and Martha's Vineyard. Liz's struggle with her beloved faith is reflected in all her work.

Patricia M. Dwyer's essay "Timing" is one of her first ventures into creative writing. A Catholic nun from 1969 to 1991, Patricia's career has spanned from teaching middle and high school English to her current track in higher education administration as dean, associate vice president of academic affairs and provost. She plans to write a memoir exploring her own story as a nun along with five others, some of whom have remained in the sisterhood as well as others who have left. The focus of the collection will be to showcase the nuns' force in furthering a mission of justice and peace in the context of an institution that often confines and marginalizes them.

Leigh Eicke is a writer and editor in Grand Rapids, Michigan. She is co-editor with Jeana DelRosso and Ana Kothe of *The Catholic Church and Unruly Women Writers: Critical Essays* (Palgrave MacMillan, 2007) and *Unruly Catholic Women Writers: Creative*

Responses to Catholicism (SUNY Press, 2013). She volunteers in adult literacy and as a lay eucharistic minister and lector at St. Mark's Episcopal Church.

Carole Ganim was a nun for sixteen years, earned her PhD in English from Fordham University, left her community, married, inherited and adopted children, and spent many years teaching traditional, out-of-order, and unruly college students in eastern Kentucky, New Mexico, and Ohio. She has published in academic journals and has authored *Shaping Catholic Parishes* (Loyola, 2008) and *Being Out of Order* (Vandamere, 2013). She sees herself as the perpetual questioner and seeker, with the necessary touch of irony and humor. She wants her epitaph to read, "She kept looking."

Jeannine Gramick has a PhD in Mathematics Education from the University of Pennsylvania (1975). She is a Roman Catholic nun, a member of the Sisters of Loretto. With Fr. Robert Nugent, she co-founded New Ways Ministry, a Catholic organization working for justice and reconciliation of LGBT people and the church. Her book *Building Bridges: Gay and Lesbian Reality and the Catholic Church* (Third Publications, 1992) was the subject of a Vatican investigation. Her struggles with Church authorities about her ministry with LGBT Catholics are documented in the film In Good Conscience: Sister Jeannine Gramick's Journey of Faith.

Sharon Kanis, SSND (School Sister of Notre Dame) lives with two Sisters in a convent connected to the Govans Presbyterian Church in Baltimore, Maryland. Her life work—more than 50 years—has been devoted to teaching religious studies and spirituality to young women in high school and college. Currently she serves on the leadership team of the Atlantic-Midwest Province of the SSNDs. Sharon accompanies others in spiritual direction and facilitates retreats and workshops, particularly those focused on women and the spiritual implications of our life journey. Other interests include music, dancing, reading, gardening, and designing glass mosaics.

Ana Kothe is professor of Comparative Literature at the University of Puerto Rico, Mayagüez. Co-editor of two previous "Unruly" books with Jeana DelRosso and Leigh Eicke, her recent essay on the use of parody by Mexican writer Carmen Boullosa has been published by the *International Journal of Literary Humanities.* She is currently working on translating a young adult fantasy novel into English.

Victoria Marie is a former Franciscan Sister and the author of *Transforming Addiction: The Role of Spirituality in Learning Recovery from Addiction* (2014). She earned a PhD in Anthropology of Education from the University of British Columbia (2005). She graduated from the Center for Sacred Studies in 2011. Victoria earned a Master of Divinity from the Vancouver School of Theology and is a Roman Catholic Woman Priest (Canada). She is co-founder of the Vancouver Catholic Worker (1998) and the Pastor of Our Lady of Guadalupe Tonantzin Community, Vancouver, BC Canada.

Jean Molesky-Poz teaches in the Religious Studies Department at Santa Clara University. She is author of *Contemporary Maya Spirituality* (UTP, 2006), numerous book chapters and articles, including "Women at the Ambo: Perspectives of Women Preachers," in *America* (2013). Active in the Church, she co-founded *Women in Conversation,* a venue of support for Catholic women; has preached regularly in her parish for eighteen years; lectures; and at Santa Clara University initiated projects to reclaim Clare of Assisi and her charism. She and her husband live in Berkeley, California, and have two adult children. "The Chancery" is from her forthcoming memoir.

Pat Montley's latest play is *Pope Joan II.* Urged by apparitions of her namesakes St. Joan and the apocryphal ninth-century Pope Joan I, and armed with an infusion of the Life Force, Sister Joan—faster than a speeding angel, more powerful than a prayer, able to leap clerical hierarchies in a single bound—blackmails her way to becoming Pope and fights the never-ending battle for truth, justice, gender equality, and the American way by transforming the Church into a liberal democracy and saving the world from overpopulation. For synopses of Pat's other unruly plays or to contact Pat or her publishers for scripts or performance rights, go to www.dramatistsguild.com/member.

Jane F. Morrissey has spent more than fifty years of consecrated life being surprised and empowered by grace that takes her more deeply into witness and protest for peace, justice, and love on the margins of her neighborhood and world. Her own accounts and reflections of her unruly life, including its contemplative and active dimensions, have been published in various forms—books, anthologies, periodicals—from scholarly papers to the pages of the Springfield newspaper to *Gracias, Matiox, Thanks, Hermano Pedro: A Trilingual Collection of Guatemalan Oral Tradition*.

Julia Rice is a School Sister of St. Francis (Milwaukee). After retirement she chose to make poetry her new career. Her thoughts spill out in the early morning, feeding on her life as a high school English teacher, a campus minister in Cleveland, and an immigration-and-poverty lawyer in Chicago. When many were leaving religious communities, including the friend most influential upon her inner freedom, she made her decision to stay inspired by the lives of free-spirited members who found life within. With the notorious crackdown by the clergy, she found that what she thought of as freedom was maturity.

Mary Ellen Rufft is a Sister of Divine Providence from Pittsburgh, Pennsylvania. As a member of a Catholic religious community, a psychologist, and a feminist, Ellen's personal mission for many years has been to free other people, especially women, from whatever holds them captive, including abuse, depression, grief, anxiety, or antiquated Church laws. Her first master's degree was in English literature, which she taught at the high school and college levels. Ellen later earned a PhD in psychology and has had a private practice doing psychotherapy for the last thirty-five years. She has published numerous essays in *America* and *Church* magazines and won two Catholic Press Awards. Her writings frequently focus on psychological insights that encourage others to be assertively honest, socially responsible, and spiritually alive.

Christine Schenk is a Sister of St. Joseph and the cofounder of FutureChurch, an international coalition of Catholics working for full participation in church life and leadership. Her online column, "Simply Spirit," appears regularly on the *National Catholic Reporter* website. She is one of three Catholic Sisters featured in the documentary, *Radical Grace*. Previously, Schenk worked as a nurse midwife serving low-income Cleveland families. She has given hundreds of presentations and been interviewed by major media outlets including *The New York Times, PBS NewsHour, ABC World News Tonight*, MSNBC, NPR, CNN, BBC, and others. She is currently writing a book about women's leadership in early Christian art and archaeology.

Paula Timpson is very close to God. She has visited Sisters at retreat centers and spiritual sanctuaries. Her eight-year-old son is her forever muse. For more of her writing, visit these sites: http://paulaspoetryworld.blogspot.com and http://paulaspoems.blogspot.com.

Made in the USA
Coppell, TX
08 December 2022